youth ministry

PRINCIPLES FOR THE 21ST CENTURY

CHRISTINE CAINE

Youth Ministry – Principles for the 21st Century

Equip & Empower Publishing
PO Box 1252
Castle Hill NSW 1765, Australia

First published 2002
Copyright © Christine Caine 2002

All rights reserved. Without limiting the rights under copyright reserved above, no part of this publication may be reproduced, stored in or introduced into a retrieval system, or transmitted, in any form or by any means (electronic, mechanical, photocopying, recording or otherwise), without the prior written permission of the copyright owner and the above publisher of this book.

ISBN 0 9578719 10

Printed by Emerald Press
Artwork by Russell Hampson, photography by Fem Shirtliffe, layout by Maria Ieroianni
Bible reference from the New King James Version unless indicated
Names marked with * have been changed

Permission given to include 'A senior pastor's perspective on youth ministry' in this book by Brian Houston. Copyright 2002 Brian Houston.

Dedication

To all the youth pastors, leaders and workers on the frontlines

Your life is making an eternal difference

To all those who have gone before, carrying the torch of Youth Ministry – Thank you

Endorsements

■

Christine Caine is one of my favorite teachers on the subject of youth ministry. Drawing from her extensive experience, she is able to combine the philosophy of ministry with real, rubber-meets-the-road experience. I highly recommend this exciting book. It will inspire you and, what's more important, equip you to redefine the youth culture where you live and work!

Mal Fletcher
Founder/Executive Director
Next Wave International

■

Christine is one of very few women to have really made her mark on youth ministry worldwide. She has an amazing gift of communicating the Gospel. This book will give you essential keys to helping your youth ministry long term. I recommend you read this one!

Russell Evans
Youth Alive National Director
Director - Planet Shakers, Australia

■

Christine's ability to articulate the challenges faced by youth and youth leaders is outstanding. She brings clarity to a generation about how to chart a course toward fulfilling their purpose and destiny. You will never be the same after being exposed to this dynamic leader.

Benny Perez
Director- Pacesetters International, USA

■

This book is essential to anyone desiring to achieve effective youth ministry in this postmodern world. It will give you more than just the 'how to' of ministry but more importantly, it will give you insight into the heart and soul of the youth leader. Pay attention - this book will help position you for significance.

Reverend Spike
Director – Youth America

For every youth leader who's been 'bitten' by the reality of youth ministry – this is a book you'll want to read and re-read. Christine Caine has a grasp not only on youth ministry but the heartbeat of youth culture worldwide. Her practical, no-nonsense approach to training, mixed with her passion for young people has ignited a fire in youth ministries around the globe. Get ready to have your vision explode!

Monica Prescott
Director - Youth Alive, Canada

■

Here is a woman who lives and breathes the purpose of championing the cause of the local church. Christine Caine is a woman with intense passion - an intense passion for God, His church, for young people and for life. This passion has established her internationally as a dynamic preacher. Christine has been able to marry her passion with strategy and is a builder of, and a mentor for, youth ministries around the world.

John Morgan
Director – Youth Invasion International

■

Christine Caine is one of the best youth speakers in the world and has played a major role in developing youth leadership in Norway. She is a great inspiration and this book is essential reading for all leaders.

Odd Arve Roed
Director- Youth Alive, Norway

■

This is an absolute must read for everybody in youth ministry worldwide - it will change your life. Christine's passion, knowledge and skill in communicating with relevancy to young people and leaders is outstanding.

Andreas Nielsen
Director - Oneighty Europe
Youth Pastor - Stockholm Karisma Center, Sweden

I highly recommend that anyone who has a heart for impacting youth not only read, but also consume, the wisdom Christine has learned as she has spanned the globe igniting fire in the hearts of leaders and youth alike for the Gospel of Jesus Christ.

Aaron Jayne
Associate Pastor - Angelus Temple: Home Of The Dream Center, USA

■

Christine Caine is an amazing youth communicator who has for many years been at the forefront of youth ministry in Australia and beyond! Christine is well versed in youth culture and understands what is required to reach and change a generation. She is more than qualified to write this book. It is a must read for any aspiring youth leader or generation changer.

Jurgen Matthesius
Youth Director – Christian City Churches of Australia
Youth Pastor- CCC Oxford Falls

■

Chris Caine's new book, "Youth Ministry - Principles For the 21st Century" is a resource for any youth leader or senior minister serious about making a difference in the lives of young people. With 14 years of youth ministry experience, speaking to thousands of youth around the world each year, Christine will lead you to a place that demands a response.

Sam Monk
Youth Director – Apostolic Churches, New Zealand

■

Christine Caine has a unique gifting that allows her to somehow 'get inside' the heads and hearts of young people to help them realize the magnitude of what God has called them to do. She has placed this same anointing and message in this book so that youth leaders can apply it and see their young people flourish. It is a must read for youth leaders and ministers.

Nancy Alcorn
President & Founder - Mercy Ministries of America

Contents

Foreword – Jeanne Mayo   11
Author's Note   15

SECTION 1: A FOUNDATION

1. Youth Ministry - Why is it Needed in the 21st Century?   21
2. Youth Ministry - Who Are 21st Century Young People?   33
3. Youth Ministry - What is 21st Century Youth Ministry?   45
4. Youth Ministry - 21st Century Youth Leaders   57

SECTION 2: DNA OF A YOUTH LEADER

What Does Genetics Have to do with Youth Ministry?   69

1. A Passion for the Cause of Christ   71
2. A Love for the Local Church   77
3. A Passion for the Lost   85
4. A Christlike Character   93
5. A Servant   101
6. A Dreamer   109
7. A Visionary   121
8. Is Faith Filled   127
9. Knows Now is Their Time   133
10. Is Purpose Driven   139
11. Has A Possession Mentality   147
12. A Love of the Word   157
13. Relies on Prayer   165

14.	A True Worshipper	175
15.	Builds Healthy Relationships	181
16.	Lives Generously	193
17.	Builds Lives	203
18.	A Team Player	213
19.	A Mobilizer of Young People	221
20.	A Committent to Discipleship	229

SECTION 3: REPRODUCING THE GENERATIONS

| 1. | Your Church – One Generation from Extinction | 239 |
| 2. | Epilogue - Brian Houston
A Senior Pastor's Perspective | 251 |

Thank yous	255
Footnotes	257
References	258
Recommended Reading	259
About the Author	261
Resources	263

Foreword

I have served more than three decades in full-time youth ministry. This is long enough to remember when Kum By Yah was still a cool youth worship song, enough time to recall the days when cutting-edge youth pastors used new inventions like overhead projectors and CD players, and long enough to have read a few hundred books on how to do youth ministry effectively.

That is why I am genuinely excited to introduce you to Christine Caine's hallmark book, "Youth Ministry – Principles for the 21st Century". You will quickly understand that you are not holding in your hands, 'just another book on youth ministry'.

Have you ever met its author, Chris Caine? You would remember her if you had. She is one of the most unforgettable people to grace the planet in recent times. You would be captured by her contagious laugh, riveted by her keen mind, motivated by her passion for youth ministry, refreshed by her uncompromising authenticity and convicted by her determined commitment to pursue Christ at any cost. All these attributes shout loudly from each page of this text.

This book is the substance of Christine's MINISTRY HEART AND LIFE. It is a 'how to LIVE youth ministry book'. Believe me, there are not many of these on the market these days! The chapters of this much-needed reference deal with issues of the leader's heart and character, issues like integrity, loyalty and guts. Agonizingly, youth ministry conferences and seminars do not deal with these issues much anymore. Maybe this is why the typical full-time youth pastor only stays at one church for an average of 18 months. We have worked harder at building a leader's charisma than we have their character. The results have been devastating.

All the great METHODS in the world are of little help when a person's SPIRIT AND LIFE do not embody the true essence of Christ-honoring youth ministry.

In my three exciting decades of youth ministry, I have seen and heard the glamour, the spectacular events and the powerful preaching. From my vantage point, they all have one thing in common: they have all been shallow and short-lived.

I am no longer impressed by the noisy trends or flamboyant fads. The embarrassing truth is that I do not even know how to play a video game! It is hard to believe that even without this basic skill, the youth ministry I most recently led somehow grew from 30 teenagers each week to approximately 1000. I am convinced that all the skills and fads in the world do not make a big difference when it comes to building young people's lives.

Through the years, I have chosen to prioritize loving Jesus and loving teenagers above all else. I have listened intently to hundreds of romance stories, chosen to pray intently with bewildered teenagers and committed to intently seeking God with hundreds of spiritually hungry young adults. I am aware that this does not sound too glamorous, but in truth, simple decisions of character and consistency are the most strategic building blocks for effective long haul youth ministry.

It has been said, "We'll never make a significant difference in any arena until it becomes a righteous obsession." With this in mind, I have simply lived these last 30 years in youth ministry focused on making teenagers and young adults my 'righteous obsession'. TODAY'S YOUTH CULTURE DEMANDS AN AUTHENTIC MESSAGE AND AN AUTHENTIC LOVE.

There is a woman in the Old Testament named Rizpah. She would have been amazing in youth ministry. Her two sons were hung as a result of a national conflict. Long after they had taken their last breath, Rizpah stood on a rock near the place of their execution and used sackcloth to beat the vultures and wild beasts away. Rizpah's message was unmistakably clear: "These two boys are still my sons and nobody is messing with them!" Her love was equally unshakable: "Although to others, these two guys may be nothing more than smelly, decaying skeletons...I refuse to leave them alone. No matter what they're still my boys."

Rizpah understood the concept of making Christ-centered ministry her "righteous obsession". That is probably why after months of Rizpah standing guard over her sons' decaying bodies, a royal decree was issued commanding that their bodies be taken down and honorably buried in the King's personal tomb!

Rizpah gives us such a great picture of authentic youth ministry in and to the 21st century. It is about a heart of endurance and love that keeps fighting for sin-decayed teenagers until they GO TO SEE THE KING!

What does that Old Testament account have to do with the book you are now holding in your hands? The connection is very simple: it has been written by a contemporary Rizpah! I have spent time around

Chris Caine when the video cameras were not rolling and the microphones were far away. Those are the hours that you learn what a youth communicator is really all about. You know what I saw? I repeatedly saw a woman with her cell phone glued to her ear unselfishly taking care of person after person. I repeatedly heard words of encouragement and vision roll off her tongue as she connected with people. I witnessed her uncompromising authenticity that cut through 'the junk' and told it like it was.

So congratulations as you jump into the first chapter of "Youth Ministry – Principles for the 21st Century." You will soon understand why I think the Lord was smiling on you when you picked up this book. How fortunate you are that the Holy Spirit allowed your paths to cross.

Jeanne Mayo
President - Youth Source Ministries

Author's Note

Finally I have stopped long enough to type the thoughts I have about youth ministry and leadership which have been burning in my heart for the last three years.

I have been involved in full time youth ministry for 14 years. During this time I helped establish, and eventually became the Director of, the Hills District Youth Service, a community-based youth center working essentially with unchurched young people and their families. I recently handed over the reins of Youth Alive NSW; a state youth movement that holds large-scale evangelistic youth rallies and offers youth leadership training, support and development. I am now released to remain actively involved in youth ministry on an increasingly global scale.

In essence, I have been involved with at risk young people, church youth ministries, community youth services, high school and university ministry, young people in detention centers, and young people emotionally scarred by abuse, rejection, eating disorders, suicide and family breakup. I have also had the privilege of serving hundreds of youth leaders and ministries in 15 nations.

I have loved the journey. I have seen many lives transformed by the power of the Gospel, countless thousands of young people make decisions to serve Jesus Christ as their Lord and Savior, and many youth ministries grow and flourish. I have had the opportunity to work alongside some amazing people who have sacrificed everything to serve the next generation. These youth leaders have forsaken money, status, recognition and a 'normal life' to give young people the opportunity for a future. They are leaders who have literally laid down their lives for a cause greater than themselves.

The catalyst for finally penning this book was a phone call I received from a devastated and disillusioned youth leader who had just found out his youth pastor had been having an affair with a young person in his youth ministry.

Although I was almost eight months pregnant, I could not just sit back and 'pray for them from a distance'. I checked with my doctor and flew the 20 hour plane trip to be there for my hurting partners in the ministry - to cry with them, console them, encourage and refocus them. I have known few crises in youth ministry that have come at convenient times, or within normal business hours.

I saw their disillusioned faces each time I closed my eyes during the flight home. Youth leaders in their late teens and early 20's grappling with the reality of betrayal, friendships severed and loyalties violated.

I am more determined than ever to play my part in encouraging a generation of youth leaders to run their race with certainty, to finish their course well. My desire is to see more youth leaders decide that they will be involved in youth ministry for the long haul and to live a life worthy of their calling. Youth leaders who will dare to deal with deep issues of their heart and the unresolved issues from their past, who will not try to outwork their own fears, insecurities, sexuality and emotional brokenness through their leadership. They will be whole enough to lead a wounded and broken generation to wholeness in Christ.

Never before has there been a greater need for youth leaders who are integrous - committed, loyal, faithful and full of Godly character. In our postmodern 21st century, defined by compromise and relativism, we need a radical leadership generation to emerge that will adhere to Biblical values, have a holistic approach to youth ministry, champion the cause of the local church and believe that the Gospel works.

This book will unapologetically stir and challenge you to the core. It will deal with issues of the heart, the philosophy and motives behind effective youth ministry. It will provide you with principles I have seen work in different nations, ethnic groups, cultures and socio-economic settings. Ultimately, it is about building real youth ministries with real youth leaders in whatever context God has placed you.

I have given myself to raising up a generation of world changers because I believe in young people. I know that God still uses young people to change their world. Young people need role models and mentors who will disciple them to be followers of Jesus Christ. We need radical youth leaders who will dare to raise up an army of young people who will give their all for the cause of Christ. I believe you are one of those generation changers and like Esther; 'this is your time such as this'.

My prayer is that this book helps to inspire you to reach a lost generation with the Gospel of Jesus Christ – the only hope of the world.

Yours for a Revolution

Chris Caine

christine caine

SECTION ONE

A Foundation

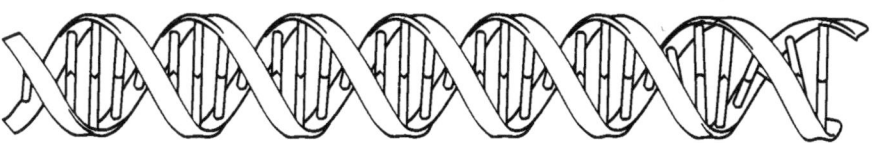

"For no other foundation can anyone lay than that which is laid, which is Jesus Christ."

(1 Corinthians 3:11)

christine caine

YOUTH MINISTRY:

Why is it Needed in the 21ˢᵗ Century?

"It is not the how to but why I do something that is important. It is the why that gives you the power to do the how to. The reason why most people do not do what they can do is because they do not have a strong enough why."

Robert T Kiyosaki

christine caine

YOUTH MINISTRY:
Why is it Needed in the 21st Century?

Over half of the world's six billion people are 25 years of age or younger. Furthermore, it is this group that are most likely to make decisions for Christ.

Research[1] tells us:

- 19 out of every 20 people who make a decision to follow Jesus do so before the age of 25
- After the age of 25 the chance of being saved is statistically 1 in 10,000
- After the age of 35 the chance of being saved is statistically 1 in 50,000
- After the age of 45 the chance of being saved statistically is 1 in 200,000

However, the National Church Life Survey[2] found that fewer than 20 per cent of Australians are regular churchgoers. Of these only six percent are aged 15 –19 years.

These startling statistics reveal that it is crucial we build ministries that target young people. We cannot ignore half the world!

It is during this period of physical, social, emotional, and spiritual transition that we label the 'teenage years', that young people form their identities and values and are on a quest for meaning, significance and security. If we do not present Jesus as the answer to this generation then they are going to endeavour to meet these needs with other things.

THE RISE OF POSTMODERNISM

The 21st century presents the church, and more specifically, youth ministry with a unique set of challenges and opportunities in reaching a generation with the Gospel of Jesus Christ.

Not since the birth of modernism in the 1750s, where scientific discovery caused people to doubt God's infallibility and believe that human problems could be solved through human reason, has there been such a shift in how people view the world and their place in it.

During the last two decades, a new way of thinking has flourished, termed postmodernism.

The following poem, "Creed", by Steve Turner helps explain the postmodern mind:

> We believe in Marxfreudanddarwin
> We believe everything is OK
> as long as you don't hurt anyone,
> to the best of your definition of hurt,
> and to the best of your knowledge
> We believe in sex before, during, and
> after marriage.
> We believe in the therapy of sin.
> We believe adultery is fun.
> We believe that sodomy's OK.
> We believe that taboos are taboo.
> We believe that everything's getting better
> despite evidence to the contrary.

The evidence must be investigated
And you can prove anything with evidence.
We believe there is something in horoscopes,
UFO's and bent spoons;
Jesus was a good man just like Buddha,
Mohammed, and ourselves.
He was a good moral teacher although we think
His good morals were bad.
We believe that all religions are basically the same—
at least the one we read was.
They all believe in love and goodness.
They only differ on matters of creation,
sin, heaven, hell, God, and salvation.
We believe after death comes the Nothing
Because when you ask the dead what happens
they say nothing.
If death is not the end, if the dead have lied, then it's
compulsory heaven for all
excepting perhaps
Hitler, Stalin, and Ghengis Khan.
We believe in Masters and Johnson.
What's selected is average.
What's average is normal.
What's normal is good.
We believe in total disarmament.
We believe there are direct links between warfare and
bloodshed.
Americans should beat their guns into tractors

and the Russians would be sure to follow.
  We believe that man is essentially good.
It's only his behavior that lets him down.
This is the fault of society.
Society is the fault of conditions.
Conditions are the fault of society.
  We believe that each man must find the truth that
is right for him.
Reality will adapt accordingly,
The universe will readjust.
History will alter.
We believe that there is no absolute truth
excepting the truth
that there is no absolute truth.
  We believe in the rejection of creeds,
And the flowering of individual thought.

ABSOLUTELY NO ABSOLUTES

Postmodern thinking is underwritten by skepticism. The key characteristics of postmodern thinking are:

1. There are no absolutes; everything is relative.
   Translation: "What I do and believe is up to me."

2. Subjective experience supersedes logic and objective facts.
   Translation: "I choose what I believe based on what makes me feel comfortable and good."

3. The nature of Truth and God are relative not absolute.
   Translation: "You have your God, I will have mine, just don't try to convert me."

Seventy per cent of this generation believe there is no absolute truth[3] (apart from their belief that there are no absolutes!) They claim that truth is relative and personal.

In his book **Girlfriend in a Coma**, Douglas Coupland summarizes this generation in this way:

"We really don't seem to have any values, any absolutes. We've always manoeuvred our values to suit our immediate purposes. There's nothing large in our lives…instead of serving a higher purpose we've always been more concerned with developing our personalities and being free…what evidence do we have of inner lives, of acts of kindness, evidence of contemplation, devotion, sacrifice? All these things indicate a world inside us…"

The essence of the Gospel message is totally opposite to postmodernist thinking; it is based on absolute truth. Jesus said, *"I am the way, the truth, the life. No one comes to the Father except through Me."* (John 14:6) He did not give a range of options for getting to God, He presented Himself as the only means of salvation.

The challenge for the 21st century youth leader is to present this absolute truth to a generation who believe all things are relative.

Proclaiming an absolute message in a relative world can be both a challenge and an opportunity. Contrary to popular opinion, young people across the globe are searching for truth, meaning, significance, security and unconditional love. As Christians, we know the source of all truth and love and we can offer people a life of eternal significance through Jesus Christ.

We must ensure that we understand our world to reach our world. We should communicate in a way that this generation understands and be mindful of the fact that their worldview does not generally encompass eternity or have a God framework.

LIFE MEANS WHAT?

I remember sitting through numerous science classes at school where the teachers tried to convince us that in the beginning there was nothing. Then nothing collided with nothing and something was formed: the cockroach. It had a genetic mutation and subsequently, the frog evolved. After a while the frog genetically mutated and there evolved an ape. The ape was walking around the planet one hot summer's day and went to the hairdresser, had a cut, shave and blow dry, and here we are today. Admittedly none of the teachers put it quite like that, but that is how my overactive imagination interpreted this theory.

In its various forms, the theory of evolution has caused people to believe the fundamental lie that we have evolved from a meaningless random series of events originating from a cosmic 'big bang'. That is, we came from nothing, we live for no apparent reason, and we are going nowhere.

If we tell a generation long enough there is no ultimate purpose for their life, invariably they will begin to live like they have no future.

The devil has launched an attack on this generation and blinded them to the Truth to prevent them from choosing to follow Jesus. We hear horror stories about students killing students, young people addicted to alcohol and other drugs, young men and women who use sex to meet their emotional needs and those young people who decide it is all too much and decide to take their own lives.

Our youth ministries have a vital role to play in reaching this generation with the Truth that a God who loves them created them with purpose and a destiny.

NO CONSEQUENCES

21st Century young people have been raised in a society where the distinction between right and wrong has been grossly diluted.

Movie stars, rock stars and sports stars have replaced God as a moral compass. Television, the big screen and radio deliver the sermons that frame their worldview. Social, political and educational policies have bowed to political correctness, encouraging youth not only to accept ungodly practices, but, at times, to celebrate them.

This has resulted in a generation that lacks a true source of strength with which to live, goodness by which to live and freedom in which to live.

I was powerfully reminded of this reality after speaking at a youth conference in Victoria, Australia. I had just finished telling my story when a young girl named Rachel* came to talk to me.

"Excuse me Chris, do you have a few minutes?" I turned to see a very nervous 19-year-old standing behind me, waiting to be invited to sit down.

My heart melted as I saw the deep pain in her eyes. We started to talk about life, boys, dreams, boys, the camp, and, you guessed it, boys.

I quickly established that Rachel was not a Christian and that her mother 'forced' her to come to the conference. She had lived a wild life for someone so young, and the scars of rejection, bitterness, hurt and loneliness were already evident.

After about an hour, Rachel stated, "I had an abortion two weeks ago, and my boyfriend has left me." As we talked for a while longer, I realized her main concern was not the fact she had aborted a child, but rather, that she no longer had a boyfriend. I asked her, "Rachel, do you think you did anything wrong when you had the abortion?" She looked at me like I was crazy. "Of course not! What else could I have done? After all, I really want to travel."

I am not suggesting that all young people hold Rachel's view about abortion. Her story does, however, provide us with insight into a generation that has little point of reference for distinguishing between right and wrong.

Some of you may be thinking, "What is the use? Can our youth ministry really make a difference?" I truly believe the answer is 'yes'. Jesus is the same yesterday, today and forever. It is His power we can rely on. In fact, the hope of the planet is Jesus Christ. Ultimately, only He can instil hope, value and purpose upon an empty and devalued generation.

youth ministry

> **KEY**
>
> We cannot ignore young people or consider them too hard to reach because we do not understand them or the world that is shaping them. God wants young people to come into true relationship with Him and He has put into our hand a vehicle to help us achieve this - youth ministry.
>
> Despite the rapidly changing world we live in, we need to recognize that now is our chance to reach this generation. Let's keep the 'why' of youth ministry firmly before us, and purpose in our hearts to make a difference in the lives of young people.

christine caine

YOUTH MINISTRY:

Who Are 21st Century Young People?

"Youth culture is worldwide- kids are watching the same movies, the same videos, listening to the same music, wearing the same clothes, making the same mistakes and desperately needing the same Savior. Young people are tormented by loneliness, saturated by sex, fascinated with the dark side of the supernatural, and susceptible to suicide. We cannot abandon them."

Ron Hutchcraft

christine caine

YOUTH MINISTRY:
Who Are 21ˢᵗ Century Young People?

This generation has been born into one of the most dynamic periods of cultural, economic, political, social and technological development in human history. For this generation, change is the air they breathe.

They are the most media stimulated and the most highly educated generation in history. They have grown up in a global economy as part of the global village with technology as its power source. They have lived with multiculturalism and expect equal pay for equal work. They have witnessed the horrors and successes of humanity, mostly via their TV and computer screens. They have been so saturated by mass media that image is now everything. They prefer e-mail and voicemail to personal interaction, and search the web rather than go to the library. They accept diversity and change and love having options. Marriage, parenthood, study and career come later in life, if at all.

UNDERSTANDING 21ˢᵀ CENTURY YOUTH CULTURE

As youth leaders, we must understand 'who' our youth ministries are trying to reach. Ensure that you are familiar with the physical, intellectual, emotional, social and spiritual changes that young people experience as they transition from childhood to adulthood. There are many great resources that can help you understand the role you can play in guiding young people through these often tumultuous years.

My intention is not to provide a thorough explanation of the personal development issues young people face, but rather to focus on some of the issues and trends unique to growing up in a postmodern culture. We cannot separate young people's spiritual formation from the conditions unique to growing up in the postmodern age.

I will highlight a few of the main conditions I believe affect the way young people think, which will impact on how we as leaders reach them.

1. This Generation has Witnessed a Changing Moral Foundation

Once religion and the church were the backbone of society, providing a blueprint for our moral and spiritual life. Today, 'God' is open to interpretation and beliefs about God are negotiable and relative to the individual.

That is, "What is true for you may not be true for me." Many young people do believe in a higher power, but struggle to decide on which one!

They no longer want to accept someone else's faith, they want to understand for themselves what they believe and why.

Looking through the popular media, it is clear that interest in 'spirituality' as opposed to 'religion' is increasing among young people. Marketing companies are catering for this generation's interest in the mystical and unexplainable through a diet of television programs about witches and vampire slayers.

The soil is ripe for this generation to have a genuine encounter with God. Youth ministries must provide a genuine experience of, and connection with, God. When people encounter God as opposed to just hearing about Him, they cannot help but believe that He is real and worth investigating. We must ensure that our youth ministries in the 21st century are places where our young people meet with a supernatural God who saves, heals, delivers and restores lives. Young people are desperately longing for supernatural connection.

2. This Generation has Lived Through Changing Family Structures

The old standard of the 'normal' family as a married father and mother who raise one or more children has been replaced by the view that family is any grouping of two or more people with or without children.

In his book, "The New Absolutes", William D Watkins describes the shift in people's attitude to family in this way:

> "Children now live with single never-married parents, single once-married parents, single more-than-once-married parents, step-parents, unmarried heterosexual couples, unmarried homosexual couples, 'married' homosexual couples and extended family members."

One third of Australian children can expect to live in a single-parent family at some time in their life. The number of single parent families has almost doubled since 1976.[4] In America single-parent households constitute almost a third of all households.[5]

It is through families that we learn about ourselves as individuals and as members of relational systems, and where we learn how to trust. However, with increasing levels of family breakup comes:

- A diminished sense of safety and security
- A diminished sense of individual identity and definition
- A diminished sense of satisfaction in relationships.

Many young people suffer with feelings of abandonment and rejection due to experiencing the departure of a parent, and then the subsequent arrival of their parent's new partners.

In his book, " Baby Busters – The Disillusioned Generation", George Barna says:

> *"They (today's youth) expect to raise their own families differently as a result of what they have experienced, but in the meantime they resent having been forgotten by their parents..."*

A further consequence of family breakdown is the difficulty that some young people have in committing to anything for the long-term. This generation faces the prospect of 45 per cent of their marriages ending in divorce and the same percentage can expect to marry three times during their life.[6]

It is imperative that we take these factors into consideration when we present God's blueprint for marriage and family to our young people. We must ensure that we are ministering to the reality that is young people's lives and keep in mind that the breakdown of the family unit has profoundly impacted this generation in a multitude of ways.

3. This Generation has the Media as their Mentor

By the age of 18, the average person has watched 18,000 hours of television. On average, we watch more than 80 movies each year, and by 16, we have witnessed 33,000 murders on the small screen.[7]

For this generation, the media is their mentor. Most entertainment and much of their cultural framework comes from the media. This generation's worldview, including their belief system, is shaped by what they witness on television, radio, movies, video, billboards, magazines and the web.

Television has conditioned young people to a life of 30-second intervals. One minute they are watching starving children in Africa and the next, a colorful McDonald's advert with children sinking their teeth into a cheeseburger.

The media and advertisers have helped desensitize young people to such an extent that it is difficult for them to distinguish fantasy from reality. The movie plot is exactly that, a plot. Some young people use the movies, sitcoms or fashion models as their measure of what is 'normal' and spend their life trying to attain the unattainable. They want the love, happiness, friendships (and haircuts) of those they see portrayed in the media.

The challenge for us as leaders is neutralizing the images of violence, crime, promiscuity and a valueless society that young people are bombarded with daily. We as leaders can become the mentors and heroes of our young people. We can focus them on Jesus, His Word and His values and point them to the amazing leaders of the Bible for inspiration and guidance. They need reality not more entertainment.

4. This Generation is Technologically Sophisticated

I remember as a teenager when Pac Man and Space Invaders were so technologically advanced that if you had these games, you were guaranteed to have friends for life. (Some of you will not even know what these games are!)

Technology is advancing at such rapid speed and it is taking with it a generation that is technologically savvy.

I recently bought my mum a VCR. As I looked through the manual trying to work out where the yellow and red wire had to go, my eight-year-old niece quickly went to work. While I was still struggling with the manual's introduction, she had wired it all up and was ready to watch her newest video.

Never before have we received so much information at such speed. The average Saturday edition of a metropolitan newspaper contains more information than most people living in the 1850s were exposed to in a lifetime.

Technology in and of itself is not a bad thing. In fact, my cell phone often feels like it is permanently connected to my head, and I send and receive countless emails every week.

However, access to increasing amounts of information is of no value to us, and ultimately our society, unless we first have some values that help us distinguish between what information is worth knowing and what is not.

The danger is when technology becomes a substitute for our relational and social interactions or exposes us to violence, sexually explicit images or other immoral behavior.

I recently heard a story (not the first of its kind) of a young Christian guy who had just started an online relationship with a girl he had never physically met. A quick web search using just one search engine revealed more than 300 such online dating services, several of which advertised themselves as 'Christian' services.

The web gives people a window to pornography and gambling without even having to leave their home. Young people look at pornography while their parents, in the next room, believe they are doing school 'research'.

According to a U.S. News and World Report article, the pornography industry earned more than US$8 billion in one year – more than the American music and theatre industries combined. Up to 30 million people log on to pornographic Web sites every day[8].

As youth leaders we should not be ignorant of the devices the enemy will use to prevent young people from living committed Christian lives. However, what he means for evil, God means for good. We should not be afraid of technology, but instead learn to harness it as a tool to reaching this generation.

5. This Generation is Disillusioned and Sceptical

This is a generation that, in general, feels the system has let them down. They do not trust political, business and religious leaders. They are not overly impressed by degrees or position. They trust the people they identify with, usually people outside of the system who have made it on their own. In "Baby Busters- The Disillusioned Generation", George Barna explains it this way:

> "More than any prior generation, they feel estranged from God, separated from each other, lacking meaning in life, void of roots and a societal connection. In short, they feel alienated from life. They are sceptical because they have experienced deception and rampant superficiality."

As leaders, we can address this scepticism and disillusionment by being genuine, honest and committed to young people. Through our actions and attitude, we can reinstate their confidence in humanity and help them believe that there are people who are genuinely committed to seeing them fulfill their God given destiny.

6. This Generation Desires Instant Gratification

The by-product of believing the theory of evolution (or at least being profoundly influenced by it) is that the 'now' becomes the main focus. The immediate gratification of one's senses is pursued, as people do not think there is any future.

In this 'now' generation, sex can become a substitute for love, casual relationships for commitment, material possessions for true identity, and drugs and alcohol an escape from the pain.

I have encountered countless young people who are trying to escape from their present anyway they can. Carlos* is an example of this. He was in his mid twenties and in prison for the second time after spending most of his teenage years in and out of boys' homes, in trouble for drug related theft. As a child, his mother had remarried and moved to Australia, leaving Carlos and his brother in a Spanish orphanage. Ten years later, he came to Australia. Looking for acceptance, he joined a gang and soon began using heroin to be accepted by its members.

"I was in love with the drug. I then had to spend all of my time and energy financing this affair. I stole; I hurt people and destroyed so many lives including my own. You can only keep running from yourself and everyone else for so long," Carlos explained.

Carlos based his decision on what he believed would maximize his own happiness and numb his pain. He had little, if any, understanding of the eternal consequences of his choices.

Like Carlos, many young people come to a point where they feel they cannot keep running from their emotions, from their abuse, from their torment. They feel life is pointless and has no meaning because they do not know the reason for which they were created. They want to escape from the pain, loneliness and anger and are longing to be loved. They have little self worth and they are literally destroying themselves by choosing to escape through undesirable social behavior, the use of chemicals or suicide

David*, one of the leaders on my team at Youth Alive, was driving to an event in another part of our state. As he drove over a bridge, he noticed a young man standing on the railing evidently ready to jump. He stopped the car and hurried over to the man, careful not to startle him. David began to speak to the young man as he teetered on the edge, overcome with grief. Aware that this young life could be over in an instant, David was able to draw out why the young man wanted to end his life. He began to speak about being abused and the pain of breaking up with his girlfriend, the only person who had ever loved him. David was finally able to lure the young man away from the edge and get him the help he desperately needed.

David was able to prevent this man from jumping by pointing him to Jesus and giving him a reason for living greater than his present pain.

> **KEY**
>
> As leaders, I encourage you to study the internal and external conditions shaping young people. Only when we understand their world and its conditions can we bring a Biblical response to their real needs.
>
> We need to take the life transforming message of a present and future hope only found in Jesus to a desperate generation.

YOUTH MINISTRY:

What is 21ˢᵗ Century Youth Ministry?

"We're living in the age of webs you can surf on, sheep you can clone and chips you can't eat."

Mal Fletcher

christine caine

YOUTH MINISTRY – What is 21st Century Youth Ministry?

What should 21st century youth ministry look like if it is going to effectively reach a disillusioned, desensitized and sceptical generation?

As youth groups were not recorded in scripture, there is no Biblical precedent of what youth ministry should look like. In fact, it was not until the late 18th century that we saw a focused effort to minister to young people within the context of the local church through Sunday school, the Young Men's Christian Association (YMCA) and the Young Women's Christian Association (YWCA). Before this, ministry was almost exclusively focused on adults.

The first American Sunday School Union was established in the 1820s. The 1880s saw the formation of the Young People's Society for Christian Endeavor that eventually led to the establishment of denominational societies and the development of programming materials, summer camps and leadership conferences focused on ministering to young people. By the 1930s the impact of para-church organizations began to be felt. The high point of their contribution came in the 1950s and 60s when Young Life and Youth for Christ clubs were reaching school campuses across America and holding huge evangelistic rallies.

With only this brief history, what is the future of youth ministry?

I do not believe there is one simple answer. I do know however that the Gospel message is timeless and only an encounter with

Jesus will enable young people to fulfil their God given destiny.

While the message is the same, the methods of communicating to teenagers and the practical application of this message are ever changing.

As the last chapter explained, this generation faces a range of external and internal conditions, some of which are unique to this time in history.

In order to define what effective 21st century youth ministry should look like, we need to look at some common misconceptions and fundamentally flawed assumptions that people have about youth ministry. By sharing what I believe youth ministry is not, I hope you begin to seek God about what 21st century youth ministry should look like in your context.

1. Youth Ministry is Not A Maintenance Program

Some people have the opinion that youth ministry is only about providing wholesome social activities for the youth in their church to ensure they have something to do on a Friday or Saturday night. The whole mentality behind this is one of maintenance.

God did not call us to maintain programs, to facilitate a social calendar or run an adolescent babysitting service. Our mandate is to build disciples of Christ.

If we fall into the trap of maintaining a youth program or social event, young people will soon become bored and seek alternatives. The youth ministry becomes merely one of many options, and they will only attend if they do not have a better offer.

21ST CENTURY YOUTH MINISTRY SHOULD:
GROW, BUILD AND REPRODUCE

2. Youth Ministry is Not Mere Entertainment

Let's face it; none of our ministries have the resources or skills to compete with the entertainment programs that are offered by the world. God has not called us to be entertainers of young people. He has called us to take the Gospel into ALL the world and make disciples. Our goal should be to see young people develop an authentic relationship with Jesus Christ. Our youth ministries are vehicles to help facilitate this.

I do not believe there is anything wrong with using modern methods to be more relevant and relatable to this generation. In fact, I urge you to use the technology and communication tools available to you to reach this generation. Be creative and innovative in order to capture their attention. However, if the method becomes our ultimate goal, we have missed our purpose.

Our ministries need to be built on the fundamental belief that the Gospel can - and does - transform lives.

Paul said:

> "For I am not ashamed of the Gospel of Christ, for it is the power of God to salvation for everyone who believes, for the Jew first and also for the Greek." (Romans 1:16)

A person has never been saved by a great sound system or

lighting rig. It is the Gospel that is the power of God unto salvation.

I am not suggesting that we do not aim to have excellent programs and production, but we cannot allow ourselves to place our trust in these things. Only Jesus can transform a young person's life.

A program may help draw a crowd, but people will only stay committed to the youth ministry if they have encountered Jesus. The program is simply the tool we use to provide an environment to connect people to Christ.

During the six years I served as the Director of Youth Alive NSW, I had the opportunity to travel extensively and visit many youth ministries. There were often times when a youth leader would try to impress me with their music, video, dance or production equipment. They had been to one of our evangelistic rallies, seen the 'external' production and thought this was how I measured success.

I never looked (and still don't) at these things as a measure of the effectiveness of a youth ministry.

With enough money and resources, anyone can put on a good event. With the right advertising and 'hooks', anyone can draw a crowd. Conversely, it takes depth and years of hard work to make disciples.

When planning the Youth Alive events we held in the stadiums of Sydney, I always tried to find a balance between providing a culturally relevant program and not compromising the message or ultimate objective of the meeting; to see young people connecting with Jesus.

21ST CENTURY YOUTH MINISTRY SHOULD:
PROMOTE AN AUTHENTIC RELATIONSHIP WITH JESUS CHRIST

3. Youth Ministry is Not A Stepping Stone

Some youth leaders are involved in youth ministry because they are waiting for their break into 'real ministry'. They see youth ministry as a stepping stone, or something that must be endured until they can do what they are really 'called' to do.

I believe there are seasons in our journey, and for some of us, youth ministry will not be forever. However, if God has placed you in youth ministry for this season of your life, commit with your whole heart that you will faithfully serve your pastor and your young people for as long as God has you there. We need to view youth ministry as an end in itself, not a means to an end.

The scripture Luke 16:10 says, *"Whoever can be trusted with very little can also be trusted with much."* If God cannot trust you with what He has given you to do today, why would He trust you with the promotion or speaking opportunity you may be longing for in the future?

Young people are human beings with real needs, and ministry is about finding a need and meeting it. This generation needs leaders who believe in them and are committed to walk with them for the long haul.

In all of the growing youth ministries I have visited, the one common denominator stands out; the leadership has been committed to that ministry for many years. This instils trust and confidence in young people and helps them to grow as Christians. Many young people have been through a family break up and the last thing they need is to have a different youth leader every one to two years.

Many have never had the virtues of honesty, integrity, commitment, faithfulness or loyalty modelled to them. Jesus is all of these things, and as leaders, we have a responsibility to emulate these qualities to a generation.

21ST CENTURY YOUTH MINISTRY SHOULD BE:
A PLACE OF FAITHFUL, COMMITTED SERVICE

4. Youth Ministry is Not Self – Promoting

As the Director of Youth Alive, young people regularly sent me their latest music demo or preaching video in the hope that I would recognize their gift and invite them to minister at one of our events. This always made me sad because I truly believe:

> *"For not from the east nor from the west nor from the south come promotion and lifting up. But God is the judge! He puts down one and lifts up another."* (Psalm 75: 6 Amplified)

God opens up doors of opportunity for us in His timing. Our responsibility is to be faithful with what He has given us. If we remain focused on serving our pastors and the young people God has entrusted to us in our local context, we will see the desires of our heart fulfilled. We should not be concerned with promoting our gifts, our ministry or ourselves. We should be consumed with promoting God to the young people in our sphere of influence.

21ST CENTURY YOUTH MINISTRY SHOULD:
PROMOTE GOD

5. Youth Ministry is Not A Profession

Some hold the view that youth ministry is a profession in which you should not be involved unless you are suitably trained. They believe you can damage young people if you try to get involved in their lives as fellow travelers on the journey, and not recognized scholars.

I remember one theologian saying to me, "There are enough untrained people doing what you are doing. We need more qualified professionals."

When I was the Director of Hills District Youth Service we had a great level of success reaching the young people of our area through a community based youth center. We were also able to secure funding for many exciting initiatives. In time, HDYS became a model for other youth centers. (There is something about Godly success that the world cannot ignore.)

I had an opportunity to speak to governmental, educational and other professional groups about our achievements and programs.

It was during this time that I received a letter from the Dean of a recognized University in our country, an extract of which I have included below:

> "My personal view is that despite the high quality of the programs you have initiated, you will experience ongoing and perhaps increasing frustration in moving further ahead unless you take steps to get basic qualifications that are of direct and obvious relevance to the area of youth work. If your career ambition is to remain in the area of youth

> services in the longer term, I would strongly urge you to take time out to study for a basic social work, welfare work or other relevant professional qualifications."

I sometimes think about where I would be today if I had taken this advice. I may never have had the opportunity to see thousands of young people around the world encounter Christ or supported hundreds of youth leaders.

I am committed to ongoing training and development and believe we should all be equipped to do what we are called to do. There is, however, a danger in trying to institutionalize youth ministry as a profession.

Some of the greatest world changers were not professionals. The greatest of these was Jesus, a carpenter by trade. He turned the world on its head.

None of the disciples were academically trained to be 'fishers of men'. No university degrees existed to teach them how to effectively reach the lost and turn the world upside down.

Despite this, people said about them, *"Now when they saw the boldness of Peter and John, and perceived that they were uneducated and untrained men, they marveled. And they realized that they had been with Jesus."* (Acts 4:13)

I would much rather work alongside a passionate, teachable, untrained person than an inflexible, cynical professional who thinks a strategy or idea cannot work because it has never been done before.

Over the years, I have seen youth movements that have plateaued despite their leaders gaining advanced degrees.

Professionalism in and of itself will not build young people or youth ministries that impact their community.

We need to release a generation of passionate revolutionaries that have had an encounter with Jesus, are fuelled by the Holy Spirit and the Word of God and desperately want to take His message to a lost and dying world.

21ST CENTURY YOUTH MINISTRY SHOULD BE:
A CALLING

6. Youth Ministry Is Not Formalized, Inflexible and Unchanging

The dynamic nature of youth ministry means that we cannot spend our lives treasuring memories of the past or trying to institutionalize methods. Youth ministry, like young people, should be growing, exciting and flexible.

When a youth ministry or movement starts, the original visionary has a high degree of faith and zeal. They develop creative ways to make things happen and to raise and spend money. As it grows, principles of organizational management are needed to ensure continued growth and effectiveness.

However, a balance exists between good management of a God opportunity and stifling the very dynamic that made the ministry fruitful. These are some of the pitfalls of formalization.

I acknowledge that our youth ministries have to have a consistency about them. I also recognize that some youth ministries experience incredible success using a particular activity, event or facility. The danger comes only when we begin to think of the procedure or the method as the essence of the ministry rather than a flexible means to an end. We may lose sight of the original goal and continue to use these methods even when they are no longer effective.

We cannot become so focused on formulas and strategies that we overlook building real relationships with real young people, and forget to provide them with real answers to real needs. After all, this is what God had called us to do.

In every age group, we need people to carry the torch of youth ministry, visionaries who develop a simple system for doing youth ministry that is appropriate to the current culture.

In the 21st century, there must be a sense of the fresh working of the Holy Spirit amongst young people and a radical passion to see this spread. We can learn from the past, but we must not become so locked into systems and methods that we forget to actually pursue the heart of God for this generation.

21ST CENTURY YOUTH MINISTRY SHOULD BE:
RELATIONAL, DYNAMIC AND FLEXIBLE

KEY

Youth ministry is all about transforming young people's lives with the Gospel of Jesus Christ. It is about making disciples. It is about reaching unchurched young people, turning them into followers of Christ, mobilizing them into an army, and equipping them to reach and change their world.

21st century youth ministry should promote God and be underpinned by loyalty, faithfulness and commitment. It should be dynamic, flexible, growing and reproducing.

YOUTH MINISTRY:

The 21ˢᵗ Century Youth Leader

"Everything Rises and Falls on Leadership."

John Maxwell

christine caine

YOUTH MINISTRY:
The 21st Century Youth Leader

The heart of every youth ministry is found in the youth leader. In the natural, the heart pumps life-giving blood to all parts of the body. Without the heart the body ceases to live. In the same way, if youth ministry is to function effectively, the leader (the heart) must be pumping 'life' to the rest of the body (the youth ministry). Only then will it be fuelled to stay alive, function and reproduce.

The 21st century youth leader has the formidable task of helping young people navigate the transition from childhood to adulthood and guiding them through the challenges and obstacles unique to growing up on the planet today.

The interesting thing is that many of these leaders have grown up with the same conditions and pressures as the young people they lead. This can help them stay relatable, but it also can mean that the leader, like their young people, has issues, mindsets and beliefs they have to face and overcome.

The youth ministry will always be a reflection of who the youth leader is and the core values they hold. If our thinking about the people around us and ourselves does not match up with God's thinking, it is impossible to lead effectively, and, over the long haul.

Let me explain with the example of John,* a youth leader in New Zealand. A few years ago I was the guest speaker at a youth camp in the middle of nowhere, with a broken down generator, power, no modern conveniences (except the hairdryer I had brought with me but could not use) and portable toilets. (Sound familiar?) Within the first hour, a young person had broken their leg, someone had damaged the keyboard that was not supposed to leave the church, and the youth leader realized that he was not going to make his camp budget. Things were looking dim.

I sat and talked with John as he shared his frustration about the lack of support he was receiving; the endless hours of seemingly thankless work, the limited finances and people, and on top of that, the pressures he was facing at home. Basically he felt used and burnt out.

I asked him the question, "Why are you doing this and what is it you are trying to achieve?" There was a period of profound silence. He then broke down and admitted that he really did not know what he was supposed to be achieving, his life was a list of endless activities and fundamentally, he was going nowhere and achieving nothing. At last we were dealing with reality.

Youth ministry was something he stumbled into. He had a genuine desire to serve God but had no training, mentoring or basic understanding of youth ministry. He had no vision, plan or purpose for his own life and subsequently, none for his youth ministry.

During that week, I had the opportunity to have several extensive discussions with John. His discouragement was evident from our initial conversation, but the heart of the issue was uncovered over the course of the week.

His parents had divorced when he was 11 years old, at which time he was sent to live with his mother. His dad was a very successful businessman and consequently very busy. John spent little time with his dad and spent most of his life trying to be good enough to gain his father's approval. He desperately sought his dad's attention, affection and affirmation. He excelled at school and won many awards, but nothing ever seemed good enough for his dad.

A few years later, his father remarried and had two children with his new wife. John felt even more abandoned as his dad seemed to have yet another reason for not spending time with him. By age 15, he had become part of a group that was into drugs and crime. He felt valued and accepted by them. He was so hungry for a sense of significance, security and unconditional love that he was willing to do almost anything to be accepted. This group provided these things for him (or so he thought).

At 19, he almost ended up in jail. This was the turning point. He met some Christians and started going to church. He made a decision to follow Jesus Christ and began attending the youth program where he quickly made friends. The leadership gift that was on his life soon became evident to all.

The youth team had been praying for new leaders so John was quickly given responsibilities. He had little time to become grounded in his faith. John seemed to mature quickly as a Christian; the problem was that he got caught up in the momentum of his role, and while many external changes had occurred, (he no longer smoked or swore) he still had many unresolved issues to deal with. Soon after, the youth pastor left and John seemed to be the logical replacement.

His charisma carried him through the first year, but when ithe initial 'honeymoon' period was over and it was time to start the hard work of building, he discovered he did not have the capacity or character to sustain him. The fact that he walked into leadership with a great enthusiasm was not enough. He actually had a wounded heart that needed healing.

He entered leadership from a position of brokenness. His position and title provided him the opportunity to mask the hurt for a season, and gave him a sense of significance and security, but he soon had nothing left to give. He could not help lead others through the same issues that were unresolved in his own life.

Youth leadership is not a vehicle for hurting leaders to fill unmet needs in their own life. It is about serving a desperate generation.

> Jesus said, "The Spirit of the Lord is upon Me, Because He has anointed Me to preach the Gospel to the poor. He has sent Me to heal the brokenhearted, to preach deliverance to the captives and recovery of sight to the blind, to set at liberty those who are oppressed, to preach the acceptable year of the Lord." (Luke 4:18)

God has anointed us to bring answers and healing to this generation and help build committed disciples of Jesus. As leaders, this is most effectively done from a position of wholeness, not brokenness.

Parts of John's story may have rung true with you. You may recognize that there are unresolved issues in your own life. Please do not feel condemned. I am not suggesting that you must be perfect to be a leader (there would be no leaders if that was the case). We are all 'works in progress', however, there is a journey to wholeness that God wants us to walk. I encourage you to ensure you are committed to pursuing this in your own life.

For some, this journey may require you to step out of leadership for a season to allow God to do the restorative work He needs to do. For others, issues can be worked through without leaving your leadership position, but with a commitment to seeking ongoing help. However, the first step to wholeness is being willing to examine our hearts and our need for healing

As leaders, God has called us to be generation changers and difference makers. It is difficult to help broken young people if you yourself are broken.

FACING THE PAST

In my book, "I Am Not Who I Thought I Was" I explain how I personally had to overcome my past in order to fulfill my God given destiny. It was not always easy but the journey to wholeness has definitely been worth it.

I have counselled numerous youth pastors who had not dealt with issues from their past before becoming youth leaders. Left unresolved, these things hindered their personal growth and the growth of their youth ministry.

For some, not having dealt with their past manifested itself by their seeking acceptance and significance from their youth group. For others, their emotional needs were met through seeking intimacy with a young person through sexually immoral relationships.

Emotional baggage such as rejection, bitterness, unforgiveness, anger, jealousy or low self-esteem reveals itself through the language and attitudes of the leader.

We see this in leaders who try to do everything themselves for fear of losing control or who become easily angry. Some try to gain significance from boasting about 'who' they know, the number of young people who attend their events, or their latest ministry opportunity.

If left unchecked, these issues and subsequent actions can (and probably will) sabotage your spiritual destiny.

You may find yourself focusing on the outward signs of success, but God is concerned with the state of our heart.

> *"But the Lord said to Samuel, 'Do not look at his appearance or at his physical stature, because I have refused him. For the Lord does not see as man sees, for man looks at the outward appearance,* **but the Lord looks at the heart**.*"* (1Samuel 16:7 Bold emphasis mine)

As leaders, we have an awesome responsibility to impact and influence the lives of others through our ministries. We need to be willing to search our hearts and seek God on the issues that may be hindering us from being the godly leaders He has called us to be.

God wants to bring healing, wholeness and function to our hearts. Sometimes this process can be painful but choosing to walk through it will ultimately help move us forward.

The hope that we have in Christ is a life beyond our past. He does not want us to ignore our past, but to grow through and beyond it into our future.

THE MEASURE OF SUCCESS

I have encountered youth leaders who have achieved a measure of success in their ministry (remember - success is always relative) and soon after, they want to host a conference, or begin to travel to tell of what is happening in 'their youth ministry'.

We need to ensure that our measure of success is not based on attendance figures or limited by what is happening in our city or denomination. These alone do not accurately measure the success of a youth ministry.

There are so many other factors to consider: your city or town's population, its ethnic mix, the high schools and universities in your area, the size of your church, its leadership structure and so on.

The true measure of success is Christ's example. He never lost sight of the individual. Jesus knew that investing into people would yield amazing fruit. He spent a large proportion of His time with the 12 disciples, and they went on to change the world. Now that is true success.

Crowds, conferences, speaking opportunities or public recognition may eventually be a by-product of a successful youth ministry, but they are not the goal.

WHAT ARE YOU REPRODUCING?

You can only ever lead people as far as you have gone yourself. If issues of the heart go unresolved in the leader's life, they will undoubtedly be reproduced within the youth ministry.

If the leader is not free, the young people will be bound. I believe this is why many youth ministries seem to have amazing potential when they start but eventually lose momentum and die.

If the attitude of our young people is negative, then we must examine our own attitude. If our young people are not generous in their words and actions, look at our own words and actions. As John Maxwell puts it, "Everything rises and falls on leadership."

In keeping with this principle when we begin to apply God's leadership principles in our own life, the result will soon become evident in the lives of our young people.

KEY

In order to be the leaders who God has called us to be, we must remain internally regulated by the Spirit of God and not externally motivated by the approval of people. This will keep us on track and walking in our destiny.

The job profile for all youth leaders is to give a lost generation an opportunity to encounter God and experience the hope, life and liberty only found in Him.

What a mandate! The key here is to understand that we can only give away what we have received. If we have not experienced freedom in our own lives, then we cannot give this to a generation. Leadership is all about reproduction, not just accomplishment. In our performance driven, outcome orientated 21st century we should never lose sight of our purpose: to be conformed and transformed to the image of Jesus Christ.

SECTION TWO:

The DNA of a Youth Leader

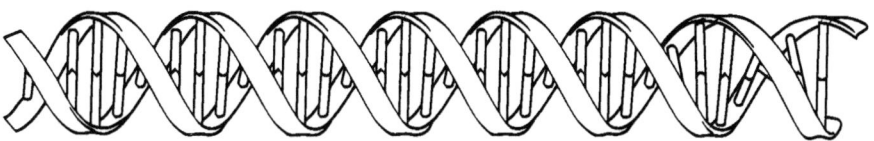

"The deoxyribonucleic acid (DNA) molecule is the genetic blueprint for each cell and ultimately the blueprint that determines every characteristic of a living organism."

(Encarta 2000)

christine caine

WHAT DOES GENETICS HAVE TO DO WITH YOUTH MINISTRY?

Deoxyribonucleic Acid (DNA) carries the genetic instructions for the production and replication needed for a cell's activities and development in every living organism. It is known as the building block of genes. Genes in turn determine the inheritance of particular characteristics. Changes in the DNA can produce changes that affect the structure or chemistry of an organism.

Similarly, I believe there are vital building blocks, or characteristics, that determine what will be produced in your youth ministry. This 'DNA' helps differentiate between effective youth leaders and ineffective ones. Like real DNA, any changes in these characteristics can produce a change, either positive or negative, in young people and your ministry.

During the past 14 years I have come into contact with literally hundreds of youth ministries and leaders around the world. This has given me the opportunity to identify 20 essential qualities that I believe youth leaders need to possess in order to see sustained growth and life transformation in their life, the lives of their young people and their ministry.

These qualities or values of a leader are not specific to any particular culture or tradition. They are not limited to a certain method or style of youth ministry, nor are they isolated to a particular socio-economic mix.

This next section of the book is designed to inspire and help you go to the next level in life and ministry. I believe that if you commit yourself to develop in these areas, you will grow personally and reproduce these qualities in your youth ministry.

DNA OF A YOUTH LEADER:

A Passion For The Cause Of Christ

"For this cause I was born, and for this cause I have come into the world, that I should bear witness to the truth."

(John 18:37)

christine caine

DNA OF A YOUTH LEADER:
A Passion For The Cause Of Christ

The phone rang at 5.30 am. I jumped out of bed, tripped down the stairs in the dark and finally made it to the phone. My mum was crying as she said, "Christine turn on the TV." I turned it on immediately to see the second plane fly into New York's World Trade Center on that now infamous day, September 11th 2001. Like millions around the world, I could not believe what I was watching.

As I sat in shock, I could not shake the thought that these people were so passionate about their cause that they were willing to die for it. If people were capable of doing something so evil for a cause that they believed in, should we not show the same level of passion (note I said passion not action) for the cause of the Good News of the Gospel of Jesus Christ?

THE GREATEST CAUSE

As Christians, we are fighting for the greatest cause known to humanity: **The evangelization of planet earth before the second coming of Jesus Christ.**

For this reason, we should passionately put all that we have into what we are doing for the kingdom.

Our cause has eternal consequence – we are offering people eternal life and hope through Jesus Christ.

For God so loved the world that He gave His only Son, that whoever believes in Him should not perish but have everlasting life. For God did not send His Son into the world to condemn the world, but that the world through Him might be saved." (John 3: 16-17)

LIVING WITH PASSION

Throughout history people have achieved heroic or remarkable feats that were under-girded by their passion for a cause.

People like: Joan of Arc, who was willing to be martyred in her effort to defeat the British and create a united France; Sir Edmund Hillary, who was the first person to reach the summit of Mount Everest; and Scientist Alexander Fleming, who spent years researching bacteria, leading to the discovery of penicillin which has literally saved tens of thousands of lives. From a negative perspective, Adolf Hitler's commitment to the cause of a 'superior race' resulted in the death of multiplied millions of innocent people.

The events of September 11 were, I believe, the result of misdirected passion. It demonstrated to the world the lengths to which some will go for what they believe. Their actions clearly demonstrated their commitment to their cause.

Similarly, as Christians, our actions will demonstrate, or deny, the cause we live for.

Do people know the cause you live for? What sets you apart from the world and tells people that you are a follower of Jesus Christ?

We should be passionate about the cause of Christ. Passion and enthusiasm are contagious, but we first must have it before we can spread it to our young people.

Here is a test that will help you measure your passio.

1. Do young people want to be around you?
2. Do you attract other leaders?
3. Do you light up the atmosphere when you arrive?
4. Do you see the good in your young people?
5. Are you preaching messages that bring life?
6. Do you dream of a great future for your world?
7. Are you raising up world changers and nation shakers?
8. Are people willing to be honest and vulnerable with you?
9. Do you stand on your desk occasionally to see things from a different perspective? (Mental note: see Dead Poet's Society)
10. Do you do crazy things at youth just so everyone can have fun?

PASSION DRAWS PEOPLE

"And the Lord added to their number daily." (Acts 2:47)

As the apostles began to openly proclaim Jesus as Lord and Savior following the day of Pentecost, people marvelled at their zeal.

Passion gets people's attention. People want to follow people who are passionate and living for a cause. Unfortunately, the cause of Christ is not the only one people commit to.

Who would have believed that someone could convince young men in the prime of their life to hijack four planes and fly them into buildings in the name of God? Who would have imagined that one man could convince a nation that they were a superior race and their service to the world was to eliminate the world of Jews?

Imagine what legacy your passion for the cause of Christ can leave in your world!

APPLICATION

Our aim should be to live so filled with passion for Christ that, just like in the early church, people will not be able to ignore it and will want what we have. Passion attracts, inspires, motivates, challenges and changes people.

It was Jesus' passion for the will of the Father that enabled Him to lay down His life for humanity.

DNA OF A YOUTH LEADER:

A Love For The Local Church

"I believe the church on earth today should reflect heaven…our local churches should echo the life, sound, peace and presence of a place where God himself dwells… they should be irresistible like a giant magnet drawing people into its warmth and light."

Bobbie Houston

"The local Church is the hope of the world."

Bill Hybels

christine caine

DNA OF A YOUTH LEADER:
A Love For The Local Church

The greatest revolution happening in youth ministry in the 21st century is that it is being reconnected to its lifeline - the local church. For years, the most effective youth ministries have been at a para-church level, but I believe that this is now changing.

When I took over as the Director of Youth Alive in the 1990s, I noticed a new trend; youth pastors did not want to bring their group to just another event. Nor did they want their leaders' main training and development to come from outside of a local church setting.

They desperately wanted authentic relationships with other youth leaders and ministries, and were seeking help on how to build their youth ministry within the context of their local church. Youth pastors were no longer looking for events to take their young people to, they were becoming increasingly strategic in who they were choosing to align themselves and partner with.

I quickly realized we had to become more focused on helping youth leaders build great local church youth ministries in their communities, rather than maintaining a calendar full of big events. Events would not ultimately produce fruit that would remain unless they were a strategic part of the local youth ministry.

PARTNERSHIP NOT PROGRAMS

The key is ensuring young people are connected to great local church youth ministries.

The Bible tells us, "*Those who are planted in the house of the Lord shall flourish in the courts of our God. They shall still bear fruit in old age; they shall be fresh and flourishing.*" (Psalm 92: 13-14)

Let me clarify. I love big events, and believe there is a place for para-church organizations, but only if they are truly committed to building the local church rather than competing with it.

Our emphasis at Youth Alive changed as we began to ask leaders the following questions:

1. Does our city/state need big events?
2. Is it beneficial for us to partner for some events, and put our denominational barriers aside to do something together that we could not do alone?
3. What kind of big events would best serve your youth ministry?
4. What kinds of resources/training materials do you need?
5. When would be the best time in your youth calendar to hold a big event?
6. How can you best use this big event to build your youth ministry?
7. How can we best structure relational networks to serve you?
8. How can we ensure that our events are not causing any conflict with your wider church calendar?

We received great feedback from leaders and began to rethink our approach accordingly. I believe this was the reason we saw unprecedented unity among youth ministries and were able to reach thousands of young people with the Gospel.

Of course, it was impossible to keep everyone happy all the time, but the fact that we were prepared to ask the questions and were not claiming to be the latest answer to everyone's youth ministry needs gave Youth Alive great credibility in many youth ministry circles.

We wanted youth ministries to flourish in their local context. We knew the best way to reach a community was through the churches God had placed in those communities, and the most effective way to impact schools and college campuses was through young people who were planted in local churches in those areas.

The number of young people who attended our rallies was no longer a gauge for our success. Our effectiveness was instead measured by those we were networking with and how effectively they were growing because of their partnership with us.

There was a definite paradigm shift. We focused on how many young people were added to THEIR number, not how many people were attending our events.

We knew our job was not to build our organization, but to build God's church.

> Jesus said: *"And also I say to you that you are Peter, and on this rock I will build my church, and the gates of Hades shall not prevail against it."* (Matthew 16:18)

The church is God's vehicle for the evangelization of the world. Our God-given destiny, and that of our young people, can be fully realized within the context of the local church. God is building His church and we should spend our lives building what He is building.

SUBMISSION: THE KEY

For too long, youth ministry and the wider church have been two separate entities. Every growing youth ministry I know is being built within the context of their local church.

A youth leader should not be building a separate youth 'church' with a different vision to that of the senior pastor. The youth leader's role is to see their senior pastor's vision for the church fulfilled through the youth ministry.

I have sat with youth leaders on numerous occasions as they complained about how their senior pastor would not support the vision for their youth ministry. It is not the responsibility of the senior pastor to get behind the youth leader's vision; rather it is the responsibility of the youth leader to support the senior pastor's vision.

Comments from youth leaders like, "They don't understand us", or "The board never gives us any money", or "Sundays are not as exciting as our youth meetings", suggest to me a 'them' and 'us' attitude which will ultimately cause division and disunity within the church.

It is vital that youth leaders are submitted to their senior leadership. To be in submission means to come under the mission of the senior pastor. There is power and blessing in unity.

Psalm 133:1 states:

"How good and how pleasant it is for brethren to dwell together in unity."

I am aware there will be times when you and your senior leadership may disagree, but this is different to defiance. Ensure that you quickly resolve issues, and that you are constantly endearing your young people to the senior pastor and the vision of the church. Our goal should always be to connect people to the local church.

Serving within the context of our local church is an amazing honor and opportunity. Decide that the youth of your church will be the biggest blessing to the wider church.

When you begin to think in this way, those issues that were causing great frustration begin to fade away. Challenges become much easier to overcome as you discover you are an important part of a team focused on building the local church.

THE POWER OF NETWORKS

I know this chapter has focused on the importance of the local church, however I believe it is critical that you and your young people are involved on some level with the 'bigger picture', that is, alliances, networks or events that expose you and your young people to what God is doing beyond your local church. God can use this to sharpen your focus, extend your vision, inspire your leaders and give you new ideas.

However, always ask the question, "How is this helping to build my youth ministry?"

The greatest youth movements on the planet are yet to be established. Determine to build one and you will find that God will connect you with others of like mind, heart and spirit. Only through God ordained unity will the earth's biggest youth revival take place.

I am discovering that God is divinely and supernaturally linking people together all over the world so that we can accomplish what no one person can do alone – the evangelization of the planet.

APPLICATION

It is exciting to watch leaders' hearts change as they receive the revelation of the power of the local church and they discover the validity of building the church over the long haul. Serve your senior pastor's vision and commit to building young people who are a blessing to your church. Remember, if you have a passion for the local church, your young people will share that passion.

DNA OF A YOUTH LEADER:

A Passion For The Lost

"History will have to record that the greatest tragedy of this period of social transition was not the vitriolic words and the violent acts of the bad people but the appalling silence and indifference of the good people. Our generation will have to repent not only for the words and actions of the children of darkness but also for the fears and apathy of the children of light."

Martin Luther King Jr

christine caine

DNA OF A YOUTH LEADER:
A Passion For The Lost

We were all created to fulfil the Great Commission. Evangelizing is the primary reason God left us on the planet.

His final instruction to us was:

"Go therefore and make disciples of all the nations, baptizing them in the name of the Father and of the Son and the Holy Spirit." (Matthew 28:19)

It is only on this side of eternity that we have the opportunity to reach lost people for Christ.

If in fact 90 per cent of all decisions for Christ are made before the age of 25[9], then our youth ministries should be our primary avenues for evangelism.

We need to be encouraging young people to build authentic and meaningful relationships with their unchurched friends at school, college, sport and work, with the intention of sharing the Gospel.

Our young people need to be trained and equipped to do this. We can help by proactively focusing on evangelism as a part of our weekly youth ministry program, and rewarding and acknowledging those young people in our youth ministries who are actively winning their friends to Christ.

Without a heart that beats for lost young people, a youth leader will not be able to build the foundation or have the spiritual resources to sustain evangelistic programs in their youth ministry. If we are simply telling young people to win their friends to Christ but we are not ourselves modeling soul winning, we will not have evangelistic youth ministries. Youth leaders need to have a passion for the lost and build youth ministries that are a bridge to a lost and dying world.

We need to have God's heart for the lost. Every individual is important to God.

> *"What man of you, having a hundred sheep, if he loses one of them, does not leave the ninety-nine in the wilderness, and go after the one which is lost until he finds it? And when he has found it, he lays it on his shoulders, rejoicing. And when he comes home, he calls together his friends and neighbors saying to them, ' Rejoice with me, for I have found my sheep which was lost!' I say to you likewise there will be more joy in heaven over one sinner who repents than over ninety-nine just persons who need no repentance."* (Luke 15:4-7)

I believe there is nothing that will keep a young person on fire for God like winning people to Christ.

If you are regularly sharing with young people about how you have been witnessing or intentionally building friendships with unsaved people, they will realize that evangelism is one of your core values and they are more likely to follow your lead.

When was the last time you walked through a school or college campus and allowed your heart to be broken for those going to a Christless eternity? What is your reaction to reading yet another story in the newspaper about a young life lost to suicide or drunk-driving, or the rape or abuse of a young woman? How do you feel when a young person loses their virginity, gives in to peer pressure, uses drugs and alcohol, or when a family is torn apart by adultery or divorce?

Our reaction to a lost and broken humanity will be directly translated in the way our young people view the unsaved. If we make Christ's final command our first priority, our young people will make it a priority in their life.

IN THE WORLD BUT NOT OF IT

As Christians, the danger can be the greatest when we have been involved in church life for a long time. We can begin to let go of our relationships with lost people. Our whole relational network can become centered on Christians and we can soon lose sight of the issues affecting unsaved people.

Growing youth ministries are those that are not hiding from the world, but are actively training their young people to reach their lost friends.

We must consciously choose to stay connected to unchurched people and as leaders, ensure that we are encouraging our young people to maintain relationship with unsaved friends. It is also our responsibility to provide them with an avenue, through our ministries, to see their friends come to know Christ.

Jesus said," *I do not pray that you should take them out of the world, but that you should keep them from the evil one...As you sent Me into the World I also have sent them into the world."* (John 17:15 & 18)

If our youth ministries are just inward looking with no avenue for outreach, we are missing the point. Our mission is to train and disciple young people to send them into the harvest and reach the world.

EVANGELISM STARTS WHERE YOU ARE

When I say 'world', I mean your community. Mission is not just about distant, foreign lands. I do recognize the value of overseas missions and the awesome experience it is for a young person to go on a short-term missions trip, but we need to validate our 'backyard mission field'. Our high schools, colleges and local communities must become the focus of our youth ministries.

There are thousands of students and young people in our very own communities who do not know Jesus. God wants to use our young people to reach these lost people. We must ensure that we do not pass up this opportunity by concentrating solely on the once a year overseas missions trip. We need to equip and mobilize our young people to live a daily life of mission.

NOTHING CAN STOP US

Mark 1:40-45 tells the story of Jesus cleansing the leper. "*As soon as He had spoken, immediately the leprosy left him, and he was cleansed. And He strictly warned him and sent him away at* once, and said to him, 'See that you say nothing to anyone; but go your way, show yourself to the priest...**However, he went out and began to proclaim it freely**, and to spread the matter, so that Jesus could no longer openly enter the city."

Similarly, in Mark 7: 31:37 after Jesus had healed a deaf mute He commanded him to say nothing, **"but the more He commanded him, the more he proclaimed it."**

Just like the leper and the mute who encountered Jesus and were healed, if our young people have genuinely encountered Christ, nothing should be able to stop them talking about Him.

It is not a manufactured or forced behavior. It is a spontaneous response to an encounter with God. Jesus said, *"Freely you have received, freely give."* (Matthew 10:8)

APPLICATION

By God's grace we have received the gifts of salvation, forgiveness, freedom, healing, restoration and more. We must take this good news to a dying world.

We should be pouring resources, time and energy into reaching young people with the Gospel. If we are passionate about winning people to Christ, so too will our young people.

christine caine

DNA OF A YOUTH LEADER:

A Christlike Character

"But Daniel purposed in his heart that he would not defile himself with the portion of the king's delicacies, nor with the wine which he drank; therefore he requested of the chief of the eunuchs that he might not defile himself."

(Daniel 1:8)

christine caine

DNA OF A YOUTH LEADER:
A Christlike Character

Young people need role-models who will show Truth to them and not just preach Truth at them. The most effective way to prove the Gospel to this generation is to live it.

Young people want to see that something works before they believe it to be true.

Jesus said, *"For this cause I have come into the world, that I should bear witness to the truth."* (John 17:37ff)

He did not say that He came into the world to tell the Truth; rather He came to bear witness to the Truth. He lived an authentic life where his words, actions, thoughts and deeds bore the same message.

Young people live in a world where there is little authenticity. The media is lying to them, politicians are lying to them, and advertisers are lying to them.

In his book, "Postmodern Youth Ministry", Tony Jones writes:

> *"Holistic: Postmodern students are deeply suspicious of those living dichotomous lives. The holistic life is one in which every area is touched by every other area. A Christian leader, student, or adult must exhibit integrity in the entirety of life."*

In my introduction I spoke of the tragedy and devastation that occurs when youth leaders profess one thing and live another. Potentially, lives can be destroyed as young people walk away from God as a result of being hurt. We have a responsibility to a generation to practice what we preach.

In a day where we use the pulpit and technology to communicate our message, we must ensure that we are the same on the platform as we are behind the scenes. That is what a life of integrity is all about; it is a life that is consistent everywhere.

AGENTS OF CHANGE

In the book of Daniel, the Bible tells us about an awesome young man who powerfully impacted his culture and society. He was not defiled by his culture but instead brought change to it.

Daniel understood his culture; in fact he maintained a powerful witness in what was an idolatrous, heathen culture. When all the people around him worshipped foreign gods, Daniel chose to stand by his convictions, even when the punishment for disobedience was death. He never compromised his witness or standards. God so honored Daniel's faithfulness that he gave him gifts, privileges and authority he could never have dreamed of. This is because God knew He could trust him.

As leaders, we should aspire to live as Daniel did. It is a challenge to stay pure in today's culture, particularly when immorality is all around us on the Internet, on television, in magazines and on the big screen. In our effort to be relevant to our culture we must never compromise Biblical standards or Truth. Like Daniel we must set boundaries in our lives.

I have sat with many youth leaders as they confessed their struggles with drugs, alcohol, sexual sin, unhealthy emotional dependencies with young people in their youth ministries, lying, stealing and so on. I am all too aware that these are very real issues which often have devastating consequences for both the leader and their young people.

Young people are vulnerable and will trust you with their lives. We must determine to never abuse our position of influence. We must determine in our hearts to choose character over charisma.

AN ISSUE OF THE HEART

From my experience, it is the issues of the heart that prevent most youth leaders from going the distance. I have witnessed how the gift that is on you can ultimately destroy you, if the character that is in you cannot sustain you.

Leadership is not only about principles and methods; it is an issue of the heart.

Proverbs 4:23 tells us, *"Above all else, guard your heart, for it is the wellspring of life."* God wants to continually transform the human heart as everything stems from it.

God is more concerned with our heart and character than our gifts and talents. Gifts and talents come from God. We do nothing to earn or deserve these. Our gift may open some doors and opportunities but it is our character that will take us to, and keep us in, our destiny. Our character is not just given to us, it is developed by us.

Caleb is a great example of someone who possessed Godly character. He was one of only two people who left Egypt and went on to inherit the promise of God for his life. He did not do this by being the most gifted or talented of the spies, or of all the Israelites. It was his character that took him to his destiny. God said of Caleb:

> "But my servant Caleb, because He has a different spirit in him, and has followed me fully, I will bring into the land where he went and his descendants shall inherit it."
> (Numbers 14:24)

God did not say that Caleb had a great gift on his life, or that he was a great preacher, teacher, prophet, pastor or apostle. Rather, he had a different spirit IN him. He was different to the others. He was not full of fear, doubt or insecurity, and unlike the million Israelites who never entered the Promised Land, he did not allow murmuring, grumbling and complaining to sabotage his destiny.

In fact, when he finally went into the Promised Land, he did not settle down. Even then he kept his cutting edge spirit. When Joshua wanted Caleb to retire, he simply stated that at 85 years of age, he felt as young as he did when he was 40, and that he now wanted the mountain that Moses had promised him.

For 45 years, Caleb stayed faithful to the original vision, not straying from the path, even when almost everyone else compromised. He did not allow external pressures to sway him from pursuing God's promises.

If there is a disparity between our internal (character) and external worlds (ministry) there is bound to be a collapse of our world.

I have seen too many situations where a leader has made an ungodly decision, and compromised their position because their character was not able to withstand the temptation. This decision has gone on to cost them their ministry and credibility. It has also profoundly affected the young people who looked up to them.

> **APPLICATION:**
>
> The decision not to sin or compromise must come before the temptation to sin presents itself.
>
> Can I encourage you in whatever you do, never get too busy to regularly check the condition of your heart. Seek God and speak honestly with your leaders about both the areas of strength and weakness in your life. Determine to stay pure and on the right track.

christine caine

DNA OF A YOUTH LEADER:

A Servant

"For even I, the Son of man, came not to be served but to serve others, and to give my life as a ransom for many."

(Matthew: 20:28)

christine caine

DNA OF A YOUTH LEADER:
A Servant

Any work of God that has had lasting significance has been the result of people with a servant heart laying down their life for the cause.

Jesus Himself set the standard of leading through servanthood. The ultimate act of service was in giving His life in exchange for ours.

As leaders, my hope is that you have made a decision to serve this generation with all your heart, to commit your life to seeing young people reach their full potential and to walk through both the good and the challenging times with them.

To be effective youth leaders we must have the attitude that we exist to serve our youth ministries, not that our youth ministries exist to give us special privileges or recognition.

As your youth ministry grows and develops, the practical applications of serving may change, but the heart attitude of servanthood is at the core of all spiritual leadership.

SHEPHERDS NOT LORDS

The Bible likens leaders to shepherds. The shepherd puts the sheep's needs before his own.

The shepherd is responsible for the welfare of the sheep in his care. He feeds them, shelters them and protects them with a desire to see them grow and reproduce.

Jesus was known as the good shepherd:

> "I am the good shepherd; I know my sheep and my sheep know me - just as the Father knows me and I know the Father – and I lay down my life for the sheep." (John 10:11)

We must constantly check our heart motives to ensure that we are serving our young people sincerely, and without desire for personal profit or fame. We must ask ourselves, "Am I building people and releasing them into their God given ministry potential, or am I building my dream and using people to fulfil it?"

In Ezekiel 34, The Bible clearly shows us about the consequences of not properly caring for God's sheep:

> "…because my flock lacks a shepherd and so has become food for all the wild animals, and because my shepherds did not search for my flock but cared for themselves rather than for my flock…I am against the shepherds and will hold them accountable for my flock. I will remove them from tending the flock…"

God holds each of us personally responsible for the young people we serve. Let us never take the responsibility of shepherding for granted or we risk losing our young people to the enemy, the devourer who comes to steal, kill and destroy.

MAKING TIME

Youth ministry has many demands, and there are times when we can get so caught up in the busyness of the work of the ministry that we lose sight of the young people we are there to serve.

Youth ministry is not only about what happens on stage. In fact the most effective ministry takes place off the platform. It happens when talking with young people over a milkshake, out surfing, driving them home, going shopping with them or going to one of their sporting events. Young people will remember these times more than any sermon they have heard.

I once heard Jeanne Mayo, say, "He who spends the most time wins." This says it all. Making time for our young people is a true act of service. It tells that person that they are valued and important in your life. By stepping into their world, we earn the right to speak into young people's lives.

You may be thinking, "In theory this sounds great, but I really can't afford to take the time to serve my young people in this way." If you want to build a youth ministry that lasts, you cannot afford not to! **Spending time with young people is the heartbeat of youth ministry. You cannot shortcut this process.**

ACTIONS SPEAK LOUDER THAN WORDS

Friday nights had become a highlight of my week since I started volunteering at my local youth center. This particular night was a relatively quiet one. I was standing outside with several members of the team, when, at 2am, Jason came stumbling towards us. As he came closer I could tell that he was totally inebriated. I soon realized he was going to be sick. Almost simultaneously, he vomited and then fell face first into his own vomit. The sight repulsed me, as did the stench. I thought I was going to be sick myself.

As the team leader, everyone looked to me for direction. Feeling faint I motioned one of the girls to go get something to help clean up the mess. She quickly returned with two rolls of toilet paper and she stood staring blankly at Jason.

I was about to delegate the clean up process to another team member when I felt an unmistakable prompting from the Holy Spirit. I 'heard' Him say: "Christine, do you see how that vomit looks and smells to you?" In my heart I answered, "Yes Lord." "That's exactly how your sin looked to me. I stepped into your life and wiped away the sin. Now get on you knees and wipe up the vomit."

Instantly I dropped to my knees and began to clean up the mess. As I did so, I sensed the Lord say: "Christine, this is what you are going to spend your life doing - wiping up the vomit off a lost and broken generation."

It was while wiping up the vomit back in 1989, that I made a conscious decision to spend my life helping others find answers in Christ.

I was reminded of this incident eight years later when in June 1997 I was approached to do an interview for the Australian Rolling Stone Magazine. They wanted to feature one of our Youth Alive rallies in their next edition.

When the magazine featuring the article came out, I could not believe my eyes. It was a centerfold four page colour spread, featuring thousands of young people praising and worshipping God. As I read the first two columns, I was overwhelmed by the comments of the writer. The article read:

> "Caine presents a sermon not from a pulpit but the stage. She comes across as that young, groovy teacher at school who you had a bit of a crush on. She's savvy to what you got up to on the weekend. When you passed out drunk at a school dance she woke you up and WIPED UP THE VOMIT."

I gasped as I read that line. I immediately began to cry as my mind returned to that night at the youth center. I believe that as sure as the Holy Spirit penned the Bible through the hands of human writers, He took the hand of the magazine writer that day, and especially had that line included to remind me of my mandate.

All youth ministries require people to set up, clean up, pick up and drop kids home, complete rosters, organize sound and lighting, serve supper, lock up, organize mail outs, keep financial records, lead small groups, disciple and counsel. The list is endless.

Youth ministry takes people sacrificing their social life, using their own car and fuel to pick up youth and investing their finances to make programs happen.

I believe we never graduate from serving. Servanthood should be a way of life. As leaders we can help facilitate a spirit of servanthood in our ministry through leading by example.

SERVE WITH GLADNESS

Serving God and your young people should not be a boring duty that we perform out of obligation. In fact, the Psalmist exhorts us to, "Serve the Lord with gladness." (Psalm 100:2)

Being rigid and boring are not traits of the effective leader. I know people who were once the life of the party but they came out of theological college without a personality!

Jesus came to give us life in abundance.

> "I have come that they may have life, and that they may have it more abundantly." (John 10:10).

We should not turn Christianity into a boring religious ritual or obligation. We should not try to stifle creativity and expression, but rather, we should be encouraging people to discover the abundant life we find through Christ spiritually, emotionally, physically, relationally and financially.

APPLICATION

If we want a youth ministry filled with people who are willing to serve, we must actively model servanthood and communicate its value by serving God and our young people with gladness. Serving should not be considered a chore, but a privilege.

Our young people will follow our lead because of who we are and what we do, far more than what we say.

DNA OF A YOUTH LEADER:

A Dreamer

"A God-given dream is the foundation to destiny."

Brian Houston

christine caine

DNA OF A YOUTH LEADER:
A Dreamer

Anyone whose life has impacted the world started with a dream. Martin Luther King Jr had a dream that fuelled an end to the segregation of African Americans. Nelson Mandela had a dream that brought an end to apartheid in South Africa. Mother Teresa had a dream that helped give dignity to thousands of India's poor and marginalized. Bill Gates, the founder of Microsoft, had a dream that continues to revolutionize the way the world communicates and does business.

It all starts with a dream.

When we started HDYS in 1989, we had a dream to reach unchurched young people in our community. We believed for funding from the government and businesses to support faith-based community projects that would instil hope, value and a sense of purpose in every young person we came in contact with. It was this dream that kept us going when we had our initial knock-backs and times of discouragement.

The dream that fuelled me at Youth Alive was to see denominational barriers come down and see youth ministries unite to train and develop leaders, to fill stadiums with students praising and worshipping God and to help young people find answers in Jesus Christ. It was this dream that kept us pressing on day in and day out, even when the challenges came.

Ask yourself:
- What keeps me awake at night?
- What do I think about during the day?
- What makes me get out of bed in the morning?
- What stops me from giving up?
- What impact do I dream our youth ministry can make?
- What level of influence do I want my youth ministry to have in our community?

There is a real difference between a goal and a dream. With natural planning and ability, you can make a goal a reality. A dream, on the other hand, needs God's supernatural power to bring it to fulfilment.

Dreams take faith:

"Now faith is the substance of things hoped for, the evidence of things not seen." (Hebrews 11:1)

Tommy Barnett, the founder of the Dream Center in the United States puts it this way, *"You only know a dream is from God if it freaks you out in its impossibility."*

Only God can make the impossible possible. He takes our 'natural' and adds his 'super' to bring about the 'supernatural'.

Whenever you dare to dream God's dream and begin to share and implement that dream, there will always be challenges and obstacles to overcome.

Genesis tells us the story of Joseph, a young man who had a dream. His story shows us the process involved in making a dream become a reality. We can learn and apply some of the principles from Joseph's life to see our own dream fulfilled.

1. Do Not Share Your Dream With Everyone

"Now Joseph had a dream and he told his brothers; and they hated him even more." (Genesis 37:5)

In his excitement, Joseph shared his dream with his brothers. This was not wise, as his dream threatened his brothers who soon became jealous, angry and bitter towards Joseph and plotted against him.

There are times when God will show you things, but beware who you share your dream with, as not everyone will be as excited as you are about the dream God has placed in your heart.

In fact, dreams are often aborted at this early stage, swamped by negativity, criticism and self-doubt.

Share your dream with your pastor and mentor and make sure it is in line with the vision of your church.

I believe we run the risk of thwarting our dream by speaking about it prematurely. Before we announce it from the pulpit, we need to discern who needs to hear it. We must always be mindful of God's timing, as for everything there is a time and a season.

2. The Road to Your Destiny is Via the Pit

"Then they took him and cast him into the pit. And the pit was empty; there was no water in it." (Genesis 37:24)

After sharing his dream, Joseph's brothers threw him into a pit and sold him to the Ishmaelites as a slave. It would have been easy for Joseph to give up at that point, as the pit was never part of his dream. Although he could not see it at the time, the pit and later, the prison, were an important part of Joseph's journey to the palace.

You may have expected to have a thriving youth ministry and instead feel as though you are isolated, spiritually and emotionally in a dark, empty pit.

Most of us do not envisage a 'pit-stop' as part of our journey toward our dream. Pits are never exciting or glamorous. In fact, they look like a threat to our dream.

You may feel as though you have no support and have been abandoned, that you are not growing, not succeeding and not changing young people's lives. Do not give up; this could well be the path to your destiny.

Like Joseph, we need to be prepared for the fact that the person who is given the dream will not be the person who fulfils it. Confused? Joseph had to go through the pit, slavery, prison and other testing to become a man with the capacity to fulfil his God-given destiny. Adversity helps to enlarge us. If we allow God to do His work in us during this time, He can promote us to the next level. God never forgets us while we are in the pit. He is orchestrating events to get us out of the pit and on to the next phase of our destiny.

3. Prosper Where You Are

> *"The Lord was with Joseph and he was a successful man; and he was in the house of his master the Egyptian. And his master saw that the Lord was with him and that the Lord made all he did to prosper in his hand. So Joseph found favor in his sight and served him. Then he made him*

overseer of his house, and all that he had he put under his authority." (Genesis 39:2-4)

When Joseph had his dream, he could never have imagined that his destiny would take him to a foreign land. It was as a slave in Potiphar's house that Joseph first received the favor that would later see him become second only to Pharaoh in his rule of Egypt. Joseph was not intimidated or afraid but rather saw his current position as an opportunity, not a hindrance to his dream. His faith and commitment gained the attention of his master who in turn gave him more responsibility.

Whatever you are doing, wherever you are placed right now, is the very thing that will take you to your destiny if you choose to allow it. We need to see our schools, colleges and communities as the mission field we have been sent to reach, not enemy territory ready to engulf us.

Choose to prosper where you are and God will take you on. Just as God gave Joseph the gift of dream interpretation, God has also given you gifts and talents. Do not allow these to lay dormant while you wait to reach your 'dream'. God has given them to you to use so your dream will be fulfilled.

4. Temptation Will Come

"And it came to pass after these things that his master's wife cast longing eyes on Joseph, and she said, "Lie with me." (Genesis 39:7)

Genesis 39 tells us that Joseph endured temptation from Potiphar's wife. I do not necessarily believe that it was easy for him to decline her advances. She was beautiful and he was young and virile. He could have fallen into the trap of believing that no one would ever find out. Instead, he realized his destiny was at stake, and chose to flee from temptation.

> *"But it happened about this time, when Joseph went into the house to do his work, and none of the men of the house was inside, that she caught him by his garment, saying, 'Lie with me'. But he left his garment in her hand, and fled and ran outside.* (Genesis 37: 11-12)

Joseph did not stay with her to find out how far he could go, or how long he could hold off. He literally ran naked from that situation rather than become a casualty of sin.

We need to understand that temptation is unavoidable. Temptation is not sin; succumbing to temptation is sin.

There are many temptations that will come our way, including the temptation to become proud, arrogant, self-promoting, jealous, materialistic, greedy, lustful or sexually immoral.

No one starts out with a desire to bow to temptation. It begins by entertaining a thought, which can lead to an action, which eventually becomes a habit that will disqualify you from the race. We must arrest temptation before it arrests us. When in doubt, flee.

That counselling session that gets too personal, or that hug that lasts a little too long, or the late night talks in the car with someone from the opposite sex, all need to be quashed.

The Bible warns us not to be ignorant of the enemy's devices. We cannot think that we are above temptation. Even Jesus was tempted. *"Then Jesus was led up by the Spirit into the wilderness to be tempted by the devil."* (Matthew 4:1)

In fact, as leaders, we become a greater target for the enemy and we must be prepared for it.

Unguarded strength can become your greatest weakness. The danger is in thinking you are above temptation in a certain area. Know your weaknesses and strengths, and guard against both.

There was a time when I travelled extensively on my own. I was often the only woman speaking at a conference and regularly found myself to be in an environment full of male leaders. I had to make a decision very early on that there were certain things I could not do, places I could not go, or conversations I could not have if I was to ensure I did not give the enemy a foothold in my life.

My husband Nick and I called each other several times a day, regardless of where I was in the world to ensure we were in constant communication. My staff and accountability group had intimate knowledge of where I was ministering, when I was travelling, when I should be in my hotel room and how to contact me. I also had to make decisions concerning what I would and would not watch whilst alone in hotel rooms. Temptations were all around me, but I had established such a strict routine it would have taken major effort and deception for me to succumb.

You also need to set up accountability systems to ensure that you do not give in when temptations come. Find someone you can really trust and ask them to keep you accountable for your thought life and behavior.

We will all be tempted to compromise our dreams and give in to fleeting pleasures or attitudes. The decisions we make in private will ultimately determine our destiny.

5. False Accusations Will Come

> *"So she kept his garment with her until the master came home. Then she spoke to him with words like these, saying, 'The Hebrew servant whom you brought to us came in to mock me; so it happened as I lifted my voice and cried out, that he left his garment with me and fled outside."*
> (Genesis 39:16-18)

In her rage and rejection, Potiphar's wife had Joseph imprisoned, falsely accusing him of trying to seduce her. Joseph could have become bitter and angry with God, reasoning that he had acted with integrity. Rather, he chose to continue to trust God in the midst of his circumstances and waited for God to vindicate him.

Joseph saw prison as yet another opportunity. The dream inside of him was still alive because he knew circumstances alone could not destroy it. God was always in control and getting ready to do a miracle in Joseph's life.

There are times as youth leaders when we do what we know is right, yet parents, young people, members of the community, or others in the church will falsely accuse us or our motives. I have learnt from personal experience that we must resist the temptation to defend ourselves or get bitter, but instead allow God to vindicate us.

6. Disappointments Will Come

"Yet the chief butler did not remember Joseph, but forgot him." (Genesis 40:23)

While in prison, Joseph interpreted the dreams of Pharaoh's chief butler and chief baker who were also in prison.

After interpreting their dreams he asked the butler, *"But remember me when all is well with you, and please show kindness to me; make mention of me to Pharaoh, and get me out of this house."* (Genesis 40:14)

Pharaoh reinstated the butler just as Joseph had predicted, but the butler forgot about him for two years. This time however was not wasted. God was orchestrating events to have Joseph in the right place at the right time to do what he had called him to do.

Joseph chose to stay faithful when he was overlooked, forgotten, used and discarded. This is the real test of our calling; who are we when things are not going according to our plan or do not seem just?

Our ability to handle disappointment will determine whether our dream comes to pass. We cannot allow disappointment to stop us from pursuing our dream. We need to understand that there will be times when we face disappointments in our lives and ministries.

At times, the very young person you have spent years sowing into - the one with so much potential - goes off course and throws away their destiny. Other times, the leaders we trusted to support and mentor us, lose track and walk away from the purposes of God. Don't give up or get disillusioned.

APPPLICATION

All dreams will be tested. If they are from God, they will stand the test. The part we play is our willingness to stay on track even when circumstances seem to take us away from our dream. The path from dream to reality is often rocky and challenging, but for those who endure it, the dream will come to pass.

What are your dreams for this generation? Are you willing to pay the price to see them come to pass? Are you willing to go through the pit, to choose to prosper exactly where you are, to resist temptation, to allow God to vindicate you when falsely accused and not allow disappointment to derail you?

God will always give you the ability and the strength to see His dream for your life achieved. Your role is to choose never to lose sight of your dream and to have faith that God is all too willing to help you fulfill it.

DNA OF A YOUTH LEADER:

A Visionary

"Where there is no vision the people perish."

(Proverbs 29:18)

christine caine

DNA OF A YOUTH LEADER:
A Visionary

When Helen Keller, the blind writer, was asked, "What would be worse than being born blind?", her response was, "To have sight, without vision."

I have heard it said that vision not only sees the invisible, it enables the impossible. Vision fuels us as leaders. It gives us direction, purpose and helps us persevere through the trials and storms of life. Your vision is not simply writing on a piece of paper; it must be the consuming force living inside of you. You see it when you close your eyes, you see it when you walk through your community and you see it when you look at your young people.

Unfortunately, there are some youth leaders who can see the present but are unable to imagine the future. They have little or no vision for their own life, let alone where their youth ministry is heading. In order to be a leader for the long haul it is necessary to see prophetically what God wants to do in your life and in your youth ministry, to see beyond the limitations and containment of your present circumstances to the future. Vision is future focused not past orientated; it speaks to our potential.

WHAT IS IT YOU SEE?

- What do you see for your city, town, high schools, colleges and community?
- What do you see for your young people's future?
- How do you see the youth ministry you lead?

Now consider what God sees for these. Does your vision match up with God's? If the answer is no, I encourage you to begin to enlarge your vision.

To see what God sees you must first gain His perspective. This comes through the reading and hearing of His Word, spending time praying about the things He has placed in your heart, believing that His promises are as much for you as anyone else and finally, trusting Him in the midst of your circumstances.

When you see God's plan and purpose for your life and ministry, you will do whatever it takes to bring that vision to pass. Once you have captured God's perspective you cannot settle for anything less.

NEVER GIVE UP

Many youth leaders give up because they feel that it is too hard, or that there is no way forward. They cannot see beyond the current position of their young people and feel they do not have the support, resources or gifted young people needed to grow their ministry. They see the door into schools as tightly shut, they think the community does not like them and the church board is always complaining about them. They feel like nothing is advancing.

They are looking at the situation from the perspective of WHAT HAS BEEN and WHAT IS rather than from God's perspective of WHAT COULD BE.

It is when things appear to be tightly shut up with no way forward that we are positioned for miraculous breakthrough.

We see this clearly in Joshua 6:1-2 when the Israelites were preparing to take the town of Jericho:

"Jericho was securely shut up, because of the children of Israel; none went out, and none came in (then) the Lord said to Joshua: "See I have given Jericho into your hand, it's king and the mighty men of valor."

Joshua's response could have been, "But God, can't you see it's tightly shut up? It's impenetrable." Instead Joshua recognized that God's perspective on the situation was different to man's perspective, so he chose to trust Him. He got his miracle because he saw the victory despite his circumstances.

APPLICATION

Your vision will take you to your destiny. Until you see what God sees, you will not have what God wants to give you.

However impossible your circumstances or challenges appear to be, do not lose sight of your original vision, continue to trust God and He will make a way where there appears to be none.

christine caine

DNA OF A YOUTH LEADER:

Is Faith Filled

"But without faith it is impossible to please Him, for He who comes to God must believe that He is, and that He is the rewarder of those who diligently seek Him."

(Hebrews 11:6)

christine caine

DNA OF A YOUTH LEADER:
Is Faith Filled

Our foremost desire as youth leaders must be to please God. Our faith is what pleases Him. We must ensure that we never get so experienced and polished at what we do that we actually omit the faith element in our lives and ministry.

If there is not a supernatural gap in our vision, which only God can fill, then it requires no faith, just natural planning and ability.

Our life should be lived in the faith realm, as it is only then that we begin to do the extraordinary. If your vision were achievable without God, I would have to question whether it is from God. Faith needs to be the driving force of our youth ministries. Faith keeps us on the edge and prevents us from becoming stagnant.

THE FAITH STEP

At Youth Alive, there came a point when we decided to change our approach to youth ministry. We would have a specific outreach to high school students and another to college age students. There were major risks involved, as it had never been done before. It was also a big step financially, as it meant holding two large-scale events instead of one.

I knew we needed a change. It took me a year to convince those around me to take the plunge. When we did, we packed the new venues to capacity. After seeing the results, it was easy for everyone to agree that it was a great idea, but it took faith to step out.

Similarly, when we decided to regionalize our training college, there was initial resistance. It took faith to step out and do something we had never done before. Our faith was rewarded as we took the college to six campuses and our student numbers literally grew tenfold.

When I helped establish a community based youth center as part of HDYS, we were provided with a building, office furniture, and thousands of dollars worth of tradesmen hours, for free. These miracles did not simply come from nowhere. To the contrary, we had to strategize and aggressively go after them. However, when we made a decision to exercise our faith, it was amazing to see the doors and God opportunities that presented themselves.

As youth leaders, we must teach our young people to live by faith. We will always need more finances, staff, venues, resources, leaders and ideas. Learn to tap into the supernatural realm, walk by faith and not by sight. You will soon be doing things that exceed your wildest expectations.

FAITH NOT FEAR

Fear is the opposite of faith, so it is impossible to be operating simultaneously in both. Faith helps us conquer the giants in our life and go on to take the land. The story of David and Goliath is a great example of what one man's faith in God can achieve. In 1 Samuel 17 we see a whole army immobilized because of fear, but one man mobilized by faith to defeat a giant.

You cannot run a youth ministry if you are ruled by fear. I call this the, 'what if' factor. "What if no one comes, what if there is not enough money, what if something bad happens?" Many people live their Christian life like this and never fulfil their destiny.

If we trust God and know His will for our ministry, we can have faith that He will help us achieve the things that He has spoken. It is when we try to do things in our own strength and ability that we are most likely to fail.

We must move away from our 'what ifs' to a certainty in His Word. The Bible promises us that God watches over His Word and is faithful to perform it.

WHO ARE YOU LISTENING TO?

David chose to listen to God. He heard the voice of God through His Word and acted accordingly. The Israelites listened to the giant, heard Goliath's threats and acted accordingly. Who you listen to affects what you hear and how you act.

David did not allow the negativity of his brothers to stop him. He did not try to wear Saul's armor and try to be someone he was not. He did not listen to the threats and mockery of Goliath, nor look at the natural circumstances. He kept his faith in God and stayed focused on Him, therefore achieving an unbelievable victory.

I choose to listen to great teaching and testimonies from those whose lives are bearing fruit for the Kingdom. I choose to listen to them and not to the negativity, doubt and defeat that comes from the mouths of the cynical.

It is time to take stock of whose voice speaks loudest in your life. Is it your unsaved family or friends? Is it critical or negative Christians? People who have not really achieved anything in youth ministry?

As a youth leader, ensure that the voices you allow to speak into your life come from those who are bearing fruit in the areas in which you want to bear fruit. Read the books, listen to the teaching and attend the conferences of seasoned practitioners who are victoriously living out the principles they are teaching.

> ### APPLICATION
> In ministry, we all confront giants daily. If we choose to act in faith, not allow fear to paralyze us, and listen to God rather than the enemy, we will conquer the giants we face and build the life and ministry God has for us.

DNA OF A YOUTH LEADER:

Knows Now Is Their Time

"Yet who knows whether you have come to the kingdom for such a time as this?"

(Esther 4:14)

christine caine

DNA OF A YOUTH LEADER:
Knows Now Is Their Time

"This is what I was born for," exclaimed Mike.* He was a youth pastor in a coastal town who had a burning passion to make a difference in his generation. I was so excited as I drove away from that meeting because I knew the young people in that part of the state were well looked after.

Mike did not consider this small town youth ministry as a stepping-stone to something else. He did not think he was just doing his time, nor did he see it as training for the 'big thing' God was going to do in the future. He knew he would never be in that place at that same time again. He had this opportunity to make it work and he was determined to give it all he had.

OUR DEFINING MOMENT

> "For if you remain completely silent at this time, relief and deliverance will rise for the Jews from another place, but you and your father's house will perish. Yet who knows whether you have come to the kingdom for such a time as this?" (Esther 4:14)

Esther was a Jew who became the queen of Persia after finding favor in the eyes of the King. The King made a decree that all the Jews in the land were to be destroyed; Esther was their only hope. She had a choice to make, reveal her true identity to the king to save her people or keep it hidden and save herself. Esther chose to put God first.

The book of Esther reveals how God gives each of us a defining moment. Every day we have the opportunity to make an eternal difference in someone's life. It rarely looks glamorous or comes with music and fanfare.

The things we do in our youth ministries may not seem significant, or not seem to be making a difference, but they may well be your 'time such as this'.

That moment may come while picking up young people in your car, counselling someone on your day off, sacrificing yet another social invitation for a youth event or honoring your senior leadership even when you may not agree.

If our focus is on what we could be doing instead of where we are right now, we run the risk of missing our God opportunity.

HER 'TIME SUCH AS THIS'

A friend of mine, Fiona*, was a high school small group leader. Each week she would drive 45 minutes to pick up a young girl for a home cell because no one else was willing to travel that far out of their way. At the end of the night, she would drive a further 45 minutes to take the girl home. She did this faithfully for two years.

At times she was incredibly frustrated, as no one else would share the load. She missed countless suppers and movie nights, but had an awesome opportunity to input into the life of this young girl.

She was able to pastor her through the challenges and obstacles of being a Christian in an anti-Christian world. She helped her through the challenges of her faith. The young girl really became passionate for God and started to make a difference in her high school.

One day Fiona turned on the TV to find that a massacre had taken place at a local high school. Two young people from her youth ministry had been killed and one of them was the young girl she had spent endless hours mentoring and sharing with. This young girl's death was televised around the globe. As people heard about her unshakeable faith in God, it literally caused thousands to get their lives right with God.

Fiona could have chosen to see the Tuesday night car trip as an inconvenience, mundane and a waste of her time. She could have done it grudgingly and wished she was at a different level of leadership where she would no longer have to pick up students.

I actually believe that Fiona encountered her 'time such as this'. When driving that young girl to and from cell, she could never have imagined how this girl's life would end, nor the impact it would have on others.

Imagine if Fiona thought that she would only be valid in youth ministry if she got the big 'preaching opportunity'. She could have missed the thing God had placed her on the planet to do.

Our 'time such as this' rarely looks spectacular or is in the limelight. Often, the most influential, long lasting and impacting things we do are those that seem inconsequential, laborious or tedious.

> **APPLICATION**
>
> Never despise where you are right now. You do not know the eternal consequences of the seed you sow today.
>
> That young person you pick up for church each week or the person you seem to spend hours talking to about their challenges at home, may be the next great evangelist, world leader or business person, and God is using you to train and equip them.

DNA OF A YOUTH LEADER:

Is Purpose Driven

"The man without purpose is like a ship without a rudder – a waif, a nothing, a no man. Have a purpose in life, and, having it, throw such strength of mind and muscle into your work as God has given you."

Thomas Carlyle

christine caine

DNA OF A YOUTH LEADER:
Is Purpose Driven

"Why are you involved with young people and youth ministry?" I have asked hundreds of youth leaders this question. It usually comes during a conversation where the youth leader is expressing their frustration or concern about young people, pastors or the world in general.

The most common responses are:

- "The other youth pastor left and someone had to do it…"
- "I was just helping out because there was nothing else to do and then I ended up with the job…"
- "The pastor asked if I could just look after the youth on Friday nights…"
- "The kids wanted to do some social events because they were bored…"
- "I am just doing my time until something better comes along…"
- "We have always had a youth ministry in the church…"
- "If I don't do it, no one will…"

I know few youth leaders (actually none) who were woken up by God in the middle of the night and heard Him audibly say, "You must become a youth pastor."

The reality is that we all made our start in youth ministry in different ways and for different reasons. Regardless of 'how' we started, we must know why we are still in it. In other words, we must have purpose.

THE DOUBTS WILL COME

- Have you ever finished cleaning the youth auditorium (with no help), been the last to leave and as you are locking the doors, thought to yourself, "What am I doing here?"
- Have you ever been on a camp sharing a tent with 15 teenagers who refuse to go to sleep, and you asked yourself, "What am I doing here?"
- Have you ever had disgruntled parents attack you because their teenager did something stupid? You placated them, said goodbye and gently closed the door behind them, thinking, "What am I doing here?"
- Have you ever turned up to church on the Sunday after a youth rally where the sound desk was broken and the carpet ripped, to see the face of the pastor, and wondered to yourself, "What am I doing here?"
- Have you ever poured your life into a young person, seen God do amazing things in and through them, only to see them walk away from the call of God in pursuit of a career or a relationship, and asked yourself, "What am I doing here?"

Welcome to the world of Youth Ministry!

In order to move through the doubts and go the distance in

youth ministry, every youth leader must understand why they are doing what they are. Every youth leader must have a sense of purpose and destiny for their own life as well as for their youth ministry. It is this sense of purpose that will inspire our young people to discover their own purpose and live their life in pursuit of it.

PERSONAL PURPOSE

Our purpose is always part of God's bigger plan. However, unless we discover our inner sense of purpose (why we are on the planet) any purpose statement for our youth ministry is simply ink on paper.

Some youth leaders stumble through life, crippled and immobilized because they do not know their ultimate purpose. We can only live a daily life of purpose if we have found our purpose in life.

We are designed by God for accomplishment, engineered for success and endowed with seeds of greatness.

The Apostle Paul put it this way:

> "For we are God's [own] handiwork [His Workmanship], recreated in Christ Jesus, [born anew] that we may do those good works which God predestined [planned beforehand] for us [taking paths which He prepared ahead of time] that we should walk in them [living the good life which He prearranged and made ready for us to live]." (Ephesians 2:10 Amplified).

In 1 Kings we read about Josiah. He was born in the midst of

Israel's darkest hour and was just eight years old when he ascended to the throne. However, 322 years before Josiah's birth, the prophet declared: *"Behold a child, Josiah by name, shall be born to the house of David."* (1 Kings 13:2) God knew Josiah was coming to earth and had a predetermined plan for his life.

The Bible says of Josiah, *"He did what was right in the sight of the Lord, and walked in all the ways of his father David; He did not turn aside to the right hand or the left."* (2 Kings 22:2)

God put Josiah on the planet for a purpose, as He does with each and every person. Josiah fulfilled his purpose and was pivotal in restoring the House of God, His Word and worship in the hearts of the Israelites.

God requires that we do for our generation what Josiah did for His. The plan that God has for our lives usually complements the gifts and personality that He has placed in us. His desire is that we use our gifts for His glory, to build His Kingdom, and find fulfilment and completeness through this.

The sad truth is, many people never discover there is a divine design for their life. He put you here to help bring hope to a hopeless generation.

Our role is to discover God's purpose for our life by seeking Him, reading His Word and searching our heart about what God has gifted us with, and given us a passion to do.

We can then teach our young people to do the same. Soon enough you will have a youth ministry filled with purpose driven young people who know the will of God for their life and are passionate about accomplishing it.

APPLICATION
　　1. Know your God purpose
　　2. Live God's purpose
　　3. Infuse God's purpose in the lives of your young people

christine caine

DNA OF A YOUTH LEADER:

Has A Possession Mentality

"See I have set the land before you; go in and possess the land which the Lord swore to your fathers."

(Deuteronomy 1:8)

christine caine

DNA OF A YOUTH LEADER:
Has A Possession Mentality

I have been to some youth ministries that have run the same program year in and year out. It is predictable and stagnant and invariably, it has stopped growing.

It is essential that youth leaders have a possession mentality. That is, leaders who are not content with the level they - and their youth ministry - are currently at, but want to continue moving forward and taking new ground.

These are leaders who own the promises of God for their life and their ministry, and who recognize that they are called to be more than conquerors.

LEAVE THE MOUNTAIN BEHIND

The story of the Israelites and the Promised Land gives us some real insight into the difference between possessing and maintaining.

> "In the fortieth year, God spoke to the Israelites and said, "You have dwelt long enough at this mountain." (Deuteronomy 1:6).

After leaving Egypt, the children of Israel spent 40 years circling Mount Sinai in a journey that should have taken them just 11 days. Under Moses' leadership, God had made a way for them to leave Egypt in order to give them a land of their own. In fact, in the book of Deuteronomy, Moses reminded the Israelites 35 times that the purpose for them coming out of Egypt was to enter the Promised Land.

There are youth leaders who have dwelt long enough at the mountain of fear, rejection, insecurity, low self-esteem, abuse, negativity, lust, greed, envy or doubt. God does not want us to pitch a tent around the issues of our past or circumstances. As Christians we are on a pilgrimage and this implies movement. IT IS TIME TO MOVE ON.

We will only enter into God's promises for our life and our youth ministry when we choose to leave past hurts, relationships and sin behind. The longer we circle these mountains the longer we stay out of the promises of God for our life.

There are some fundamental principles that will help us possess all that God has for our lives so we can help the young people we lead to possess their land.

IN ORDER TO POSSESS THE LAND:

1. Cut Away Certain Things

> "At this time the Lord said to Joshua, 'Make flint knives for yourself, and circumcise the sons of Israel again a second time." (Joshua 5:2)

The Israelites had to be circumcised before they entered the Promised Land. Although the generation before them had been circumcised, those born in the wilderness had not. They could not inherit the land based on the sacrifices of others. They had to pay their own price.

In the same way, youth leaders have to cut away certain things if they want to go to a new level. Our attitudes, ways of thinking, methodology and friendships may need to be reassessed. Leaders cannot ride the momentum of what has gone before, they must pay their own price to achieve all that God has for them.

As John Maxwell says, *"You've got to give up to go up."*

2. Be Filled With Jesus

> *"Now the children of Israel camped in Gilgal, and kept the Passover on the fourteenth day of the month at twilight on the plains of Jericho."* (Joshua 5:10)

Before they entered the Promised Land, the children of Israel kept the Passover. The Passover is symbolic of Jesus and His sacrifice for us.

It reminds us that to get to where Jesus wants us to be we must always be filled with Him. Everything we do revolves around Him. Our youth ministries are all about glorifying Jesus. Let us not reduce them to anything less than that.

3. Be Prepared to Keep Moving

> *"Then the manna ceased on the day after they had eaten the produce of the land; and the children of Israel no longer had manna, but they ate the food of the land of Canaan that year."* (Joshua 5:12)

After the Passover, Joshua and the Israelites did not stay on the plains but moved toward the city walls with the belief that God was going to give them the city. Once God's provision in the form of manna ceased, the children of Israel no longer had grace to stay in the wilderness, they had to move on. It was a new day and a new hour. It was time for them to eat the food of Canaan. They could have stayed in the wilderness and starved, or gone on to Jericho to possess.

As leaders we need to make a commitment to move on. I was reminded of this before speaking at a leader's conference in Australia. I asked one of the pastors, "How are the churches and pastors doing in this part of the country?" She looked at me and replied, "Christine, the pastors and churches down here are a little like God. They are the same yesterday, today and forever." Initially I laughed, and then I realized how sad her comment was.

We are living in one of the most dynamic periods of change in human history, and the one institution on the planet that should be prophetically leading that change is caught in the trap of programs, systems, red tape and religious tradition. Change should be the air the church breathes.

As a leader, there is always a temptation to settle into a routine and keep doing things the way they have always been done. Moving forward is a challenge as it takes energy, effort and resources.

Just as with the Israelites, some of our young people will be resistant to change. It is our job to help them understand that change, though not always comfortable, will take them to new heights in God.

Without strategic change in your youth ministry, momentum will slow and things will eventually begin to go downhill. It is much more difficult to implement change when things are already in decline. We need to continually be seeking God about the areas of our youth ministry that need to be changed, expanded or renewed.

The sad thing is that some leaders do not realize God has stopped doing some things the same way. They are trying to feed off the stale, dry manna of the past.

4. You Must See What God Sees

> "Now Jericho was securely shut up because of the children of Israel; none went out, and none came in. And the Lord said to Joshua: 'See! I have given Jericho into your hand...'" (Joshua 6:1-2)

I mentioned in an earlier chapter about Joshua's response to Jericho being tightly shut up. Joshua had to see what God saw to have the faith to do what God had asked him to do.

There are many things in our lives and ministries we would love to have and do, but naturally speaking, they seem impossible. We must lift our eyes off the obvious circumstances, up to our miracle working God and begin to see what He sees. Only when we exercise our faith will supernatural doors of provision and opportunity begin to open.

List every impossible circumstance you are currently facing. Perhaps schools will not let you in, you are not breaking the 100 barrier, you do not have enough leaders, or you lack finances.

Remember that nothing is impossible for our God and He is on your side. Decide that you will not be ruled by doubt or fear, but rather begin to see what God sees for you.

5. You Must Silence Unbelief

> *"Now Joshua had commanded the people, saying, 'You shall not shout or make any noise with your voice, nor shall a word proceed out of your mouth, until the day I say to you 'Shout!' Then you shall shout.'"* (Joshua 6:10)

I have often sat with youth leaders as they tell me everything that is wrong with their youth ministry and their young people. By the end of our discussion, I find myself wondering why they are still in youth ministry.

Joshua understood that unbelief is contagious. Forty years before he finally entered the Promised Land, he witnessed how the negative report of 10 men kept over one million people from their destiny.

Joshua understood human nature. When God gave him the instructions for victory in Jericho he knew that the negative, fearful and critical nature of some would cause them to murmur and complain, so he chose to tell them all to be silent. **He knew that doubt dies unborn if it is not spoken.**

Proverbs 18:21 says, *"Death and life are in the power of the tongue, and those who love it will eat its fruit."* If we want our youth ministries to prosper, we must ensure that we are speaking words of life to our young people.

I am often accused of being just a 'positive thinker'. I prefer to call it faith. After all, *"For out of the abundance of the heart the mouth speaks."* (Matthew 12:34) If good things are in you heart, from your mouth will come good things and vice versa.

Often, the words we speak line up with our past experiences, how much we have in the bank, relationships or current circumstances. We need to train our mouths to line up with God's Word.

You may be thinking, "What if I really do have doubts, frustrations and fears?"

My advice to you is talk these through with a mature leader and go to the Word of God to find His answer. Begin to meditate on God's Word until your thinking lines up with His. This is not about denial, or positive thinking, it is about heart and mind transformation.

APPLICATION

As leaders, I want to encourage you to examine every aspect of your life and confession and if it does not match up with God's Word, begin to:

1. Speak words of life to your young people and about your young people
2. Speak words of life about your church
3. Speak words of life about your pastors
4. Speak words of life about the body of Christ
5. Speak words of life about yourself and your circumstances
6. Speak words of life about your future

christine caine

DNA OF A YOUTH LEADER:

A Love Of The Word

"The grass withers, the flower fades, but the Word of our God stands forever."

(Isaiah 40:8)

christine caine

DNA OF A YOUTH LEADER:
A Love Of The Word

Some years ago, I was invited to speak at a large youth conference. I was very excited, as it was one of the first opportunities I had to speak to a crowd of several thousand young people.

I had spent weeks praying and fasting for the word the Lord would have me speak to these young people.

I went to the opening meeting on Friday night, scheduled to speak the next morning. The atmosphere was electric, and the music and production were second to none. As I listened to the other guest speaker, I realized I had never heard anyone so funny in my life. The young people were laughing one moment and crying the next. He had them in the palm of his hand. At the end of the message, I looked down at my notebook. I had not written one word, let alone a scriptural reference. In his entire 40-minute presentation, he had stirred many emotions in me, but he had not used the Bible once.

I left the meeting feeling very inadequate, wondering what I had to offer. I remember saying to God, "Lord, I am not a funny type of speaker. I am not a comedian by nature, why would young people listen to me?" I felt the Lord rebuke me and challenge me to present the Truth of His Word. He would then bring change and transformation into young people's lives. It was as though He said, "I never called you to be what you are not, just be yourself. Preach MY WORD (in a language that young people can understand, of course) and I will do the rest." I felt the heaviness lift off me. I was determined to just be me and do my best for God.

I walked in the next morning feeling nervous. I began to teach and noticed that as I turned to the Scripture and made it relatable to their world and lives, the young people were captivated. In fact, I deliberately used few stories in that meeting. Although I understand the power of a story and almost always use them when I preach, I felt led just to keep to the Word and its application.

What followed astounded me and actually transformed the way I taught. I opened up the altar for ministry and young people flowed to the front by the hundreds. They were on their knees weeping, there was no music and no one prayed for them, but three hours later they were still there.

It was on that night that the reality of this Scripture hit me: *"So shall my word be that goes forth from my mouth; It shall not return to me void, But it shall accomplish what I please, and it shall prosper in the thing for which I sent it."* (Isaiah 55:11)

I realized that it is the Word of God that changes people's lives and transforms hearts. We do need to be relateable when we teach young people, we need to use examples that are relevant to them and we need to be practical, but above all else; we need to teach the Word of God.

This is the most entertained generation in history. This can make us feel pressured to try to entertain when we preach and minister. However, we must ensure that we are not so bent on entertaining messages that we compromise God's Word.

A BIBLICALLY ILLITERATE GENERATION

There are many young people who attend Christian youth ministries, yet are still profoundly illiterate Biblically. It is not just the students outside of the church walls who are ignorant about the God of Israel, the story of Moses or the teachings of Jesus. The same can be said of many of the youth in our ministries.

If young people lack a genuine understanding of the Bible, they often have a superficial understanding of the Christian life. They often respond to a message and say "yes" to Jesus, but do not understand that this decision is about transformation and lifestyle. It's about saying no to things such as lying, pre-marital sex and drugs, and choosing to live your life for Christ.

God's Word is a manual for life, but many young people do not know how to read it. As leaders, we are responsible for teaching from God's Word in a practical way that can be applied to a young person's daily life.

LIVE THE WORD

"In the beginning was the Word, and the Word was with God, and the Word was God." (John 1:1)

God and His Word are inseparable. He is the Word and He reveals Himself through it. If we as leaders do not have a passion for God's Word then it follows that our young people will not.

How much time do you daily spend in God's Word? Do you prepare messages from the Bible or just throw together some stories and principles and hope for the best? It is essential that we model consistent Bible study to the young people we lead.

I have seen youth pastors who have hidden behind their gift to get them through a message. I have been with youth pastors who have proudly proclaimed their lack of theological knowledge or understanding of the Bible as if this was an asset and made them more relateable to youth. I actually believe it has more to do with laziness.

If we want to produce fruit that remains we must teach from the Bible.

TEACH THEM TO LOVE THE WORD

I am not suggesting that we need to be teaching an in depth series on the Levitical Priesthood or that we get caught up in obscure doctrines or pet theologies. Young people do not need to know whether you believe in post, mid or pre tribulation! What they do need to know is how to read the Bible and how to pray. They need to learn about faith, relationships, families, worship, forgiveness, attitudes, giving, gifts of the Spirit and how to cope with divorce, peer pressure and sexuality. They need to know that God's Word is full of Truth pertaining to the issues they face everyday.

Funny stories and anecdotes have a place, but it is only God's Word that remains forever. Conversely, we cannot be so boring and long winded when preaching God's Word that young people switch off and cannot wait to leave.

Our goal should always be to direct young people to Jesus through his Word. If youth leaders love the Bible and talk about what God is teaching them through His Word, young people will catch this enthusiasm.

We do not need to speak fluent Hebrew or Greek, we just need to be passionate about the Bible, and be a student of the Scriptures. We must embrace it as an essential part of our lives, not something to be endured.

God did not merely give us His Word for information, but for transformation. We need to teach our young people scriptural Truth in a way that impacts their daily life.

KEEP THE WORD PURE

We must ensure that we do not water down Biblical Truth to better 'relate' to young people negotiating a postmodern world. God's Word is very clear about promiscuity, homosexuality, divorce, drunkenness, lying and gossip.

If we feel uncomfortable about teaching God's Truth because of the relative 21st century world we live in, we will never see lasting change in our young people.

We must present the Truth in love, but we must never water down the Word in an attempt not to offend. The Gospel is the Gospel and we are commanded to preach it.

There are times when God's Word challenges and disciplines us. The Word 'cuts away' what is not of God as part of the process of transformation.

> *"For the Word of God is living and powerful, and sharper than any two-edged sword, piercing even to the division of soul and spirit, and of joints and marrow, and is a discerner of the thoughts and intents of the heart."* (Hebrews 4:12)

The Truth is not always easy to digest, but those who hear it and adopt it into their lives will be sustained by God and grow strong.

I am not saying that you cannot adopt creative methods to teach the Word. In a world where young people are accustomed to special effects and multimedia, we need to make Biblical Truth engaging.

We need to use language that is common in meaning to both teacher and student and continually check that we do not speak to them in 'Christianese'. Also encourage young people to use a Bible translation they understand.

APPLICATION

Our aim should be to equip students for the long haul and to help them develop a faith that survives separation from the umbilical cord of the youth ministry. This will only happen if we get them connected to Jesus through His Word. As leaders, we want to see our young people independently growing in their knowledge of the Word, not just waiting for a youth meeting to open their Bible. We want them to fall in love with the Word and to be seeking God through it.

DNA OF A YOUTH LEADER:

Relies On Prayer

"Give me 100 preachers who fear nothing but sin, and desire nothing but God, and I care not a straw whether they be clergy or laymen, such alone will shake the gates of hell and set up the Kingdom of Heaven on earth. God does nothing but in answer to prayer."

John Wesley

christine caine

DNA OF A YOUTH LEADER:
Relies On Prayer

I was scheduled to speak at a leader's meeting in Singapore and had been looking forward to it for weeks. The church where I was going to be ministering had grown from zero to multiplied thousands in only a few years. It was a young church with a passion for soul winning.

My husband Nick and I turned up to the meeting and the pastor welcomed us. He said there would be 15 minutes of prayer before I would speak. I was expecting a typical pre-service prayer meeting but I was shocked at the fact that several hundred leaders turned up. Suddenly, everyone began to pray. I felt a strong physical surge from behind and began to shake. I had never been in such an 'electric' environment. These people were praying with fervor and passion, led by their pastor.

The words of C.H.Spurgeon resounded in my ears, *"Whenever God determines to do a great work, He first sets his people to pray."*

THE BATTLE IS SPIRITUAL

"For we do not wrestle against flesh and blood, but against principalities, against powers, against the rulers of the darkness of this age, against spiritual hosts of wickedness in the heavenly places." (Ephesians 6:12)

As there is such strong opposition to the Gospel in Asia, these people were aware that they were in a spiritual battle and they knew, just as Paul did, the power of prayer as a weapon in defeating the enemy.

> "Praying always with all prayer and supplication in the Spirit, being watchful to this end with all perseverance and supplication for all the saints." (Ephesians 6:18)

They went to prayer with the same militancy that one would go to war. They were desperate to save a generation and to see all false gods and idols removed from their land.

As I stood there in God's undeniable presence I began to think of many western youth ministries that often have a token commitment to prayer. Prayer is more of an afterthought, ("Maybe someone should pray") rather than about a deep seeded desire to see God's will done ("We need to pray").

The enemy recognizes the power of prayer and therefore proactively seeks to prevent us from praying. He will orchestrate events to make us think we are too busy, tired or disappointed to pray. If the devil can stop us from praying then he is able to stop our lives and ministries from moving forward.

THE POWER OF PRAYER

If we grasped the power of prayer, we would never hold back from praying, and we would more readily incorporate it as an integral part of our youth ministries. After all, it is through prayer that God makes the impossible possible.

Some people think that prayer is not necessary because God's will shall come to pass and He knows His will better than we do. Throughout Scripture we see that God works through the prayers of His people.

Prayer miraculously releases God to do what He already wants to do. We partner with Him through prayer.

Jesus said, *"And I will give you the keys of the Kingdom of Heaven, and whatever you bind on earth will be bound in heaven, and whatever you loose on earth will be loosed in Heaven."* (Matthew 16:19)

Matthew 21:22 tells that we should expect God to respond to our prayers. *"And whatever things you ask in prayer, believing, you will receive."*

We need to see what God sees for our lives and youth ministries and then ask Him to do that which He has purposed. Learn to ask God for answers, direction and keys for your youth ministry.

PRAYER IS CRITICAL

If prayer is not important, why does the Bible tell us to, *"pray without ceasing"* (1 Thessalonians 5:17)? Jesus Himself considered prayer to be so critical that He taught us how to pray in Matthew 6:9-13:

> *"In this manner, therefore, pray: Our Father in heaven, Hallowed be Your name,*
> *Your Kingdom come. Your will be done on earth as it is in heaven. Give us this day our daily bread. And forgive us our debts, as we forgive our debtors. And do not lead us into temptation, but deliver us from the evil one. For Yours is the Kingdom and the power and the glory forever. Amen"*

Jesus actually spent entire nights praying (Luke 6:12) so it was obviously a priority in His life. Prayer under-girded everything Jesus did. Surely then our lives and ministries must be founded on prayer. How else can we know the will, plan and purpose of God for our life and ministry?

We need to be people of prayer because prayer:

- Transforms us
- Gets the attention of God
- Changes the spiritual atmosphere
- Results in people being healed and delivered
- Brings breakthrough
- Gives us God's perspective and heart
- Stills our soul and re-establishes our priorities
- Helps to prevent us from falling into temptation
- Builds intimacy with God

IT STARTS WITH ME

We must be people of prayer before we can expect to have praying youth ministries. Young people do not want to hear sermons about prayer or be told that they should be praying more; they need to have a lifestyle of prayer modelled to them by their leaders.

It would be presumptuous of us to think that effective youth ministries come by having a great vision, strategy, program and production. We need to be totally God dependent and prayer dependent.

ENJOYED NOT ENDURED

Many of us cringe at the concept of another meeting, especially a prayer meeting. I grew up in an extremely religious environment. For me, prayer time was a great chance to go to sleep! I seriously did not know anyone who really prayed or actually enjoyed praying. I had not been taught, and therefore did not understand, the power of prayer. It was a religious ritual to be endured, not a life giving force to be enjoyed.

Prayer is not a passive exercise. It is an active relationship with the Creator of the universe. It should not be ritualistic or boring but rather, creative and dynamic.

Think about this for a moment: the line of communication between you and God is open. You have the ear of the all-knowing and all-powerful God! Let's never take this awesome privilege for granted.

STANDING IN THE GAP

Do you speak to God about your young people and your youth ministry more than you talk to other people about them?

God wants us to stand in the gap for the young people of our nations, cities and towns.

Ezekiel 22:30 says, *"And I searched for a man among them who should build up the wall and stand in the gap before Me for the land, that I should not destroy it, but I found no-one."*

We are not just called to run great programs. God wants us to go to battle for the very souls and destinies of our young people. This can only be done through prayer.

There are many times in our lives and ministries when we simply do not know what else to do in our natural strength. It may seem as though we are out of ideas, or finance, or that one of our young people has walked away from God for forever.

I urge you to pray, even if you are unsure of what to pray. Begin to open your mouth and ask God for direction, wisdom, strength and answers.

There have been numerous times that I have gone to God asking Him for divine intervention or a supernatural answer. Because I prayed I saw profound and miraculous breakthrough in people's lives and my circumstances.

Some keys to effective prayer are:

1. Pray in the name of Jesus (John 14:12)
2. Pray with confidence (Hebrews 4:16)
3. Pray expecting an answer (Mark 11:23-24, Luke 11.9-10, John 14:12-14)
4. Pray specifically (James 4:2)
5. Pray believing for good things:
    - God wants to prosper (Psalm 35:27)
    - God wants to heal (Psalm 103.3)
    - God wants to save (2 Peter 3:9)
    - God wants to restore (Romans 5:11)
    - God wants to bless (Galatians 3:26-29)
    - God wants us to be fruitful (Genesis 1:28)
6. Pray with thanksgiving (Philemon 4:16)
7. Pray with persistence (1 Thessalonians 5:17)

That night in Singapore changed my attitude toward prayer. I saw the growth, multiplication and breakthrough that the church was experiencing, not just because of an awesome program, but because of their absolute reliance on God through prayer.

> ### APPLICATION
> We need to be leaders who are committed to praying, as the young people of our nations are dependent on our prayers. God is willing to answer if we dare to ask Him.

christine caine

DNA OF A YOUTH LEADER:

A True Worshipper

"We're dealing with a culture of TV babies. They can watch, do their homework and listen to music all at the same time. The strongest appeal you can make is... emotionally. If you can get their emotions going, [make them] forget their logic, you've got 'em. At MTV we don't shoot for the 14 year olds, we own them."

Robert Pittman- Founder and Chairman MTV

christine caine

DNA OF A YOUTH LEADER:
A True Worshipper

I was sipping a latte at one of my favorite cafes by the beach and I felt a thundering vibration. Soon after, a group of teenagers walked past holding a stereo that was blaring the latest chart hit.

As I left the cafe, there at the set of lights, a group of college students had music screaming from their car, oblivious to everything but the song.

This generation's love of music has earnt them the label of the 'MTV generation'.

A study by the Parents' Music Resource Center found that the average teenager listens to between four and six hours of music a day.

Music is everywhere. It entertains us, excites us, relaxes us, moves us and influences us. Music defines and shapes youth culture all over the world. Song lyrics, music videos and the lifestyle of rock stars portrayed in the media have the power to affect the values, attitudes and behavior of young people.

Unfortunately the prominent themes in most secular music are sexual promiscuity, sexual perversion, violence, substance abuse, the occult, rebellion and hoplessness.

This was never God's intention for music. It was designed for the praise and worship of God, and as an expression of His majesty. Therefore, it is vital that music is a key part of our youth ministries.

Music has been an integral part of the history of the church. It has the power to connect people with God and bring them into His presence.

It is able to influence and impact a generation. From my experience, it is those youth ministries that have established the praise and worship of God as a foundation that are making a difference in the lives of their young people and communities.

PRAISE & WORSHIP IS NOT AN OPTION

I have come across some youth pastors who think praise and worship are irrelevant and outdated. They sincerely believe that unchurched young people cannot relate to it and churched youth are bored by it.

They obviously have not tapped into the life transfoming power of praise and worship.

I have been in meetings in many nations, and watched thousands of young people reach out to God through praise and worship. I have seen how this dramatically changes the atmosphere of an event. Praise and worship ushers in the presence of God and releases the power of God to save, heal and restore.

I believe people more readily respond to the message of salvation if the soil of their heart has been ploughed with praise and worship.

Youth Alive is a movement committed to youth praise and worship. We have seen the lives of thousands of unchurched teenagers powerfully impacted by being exposed to young people worshipping God.

I have discovered as young people write songs from their heart expressing their love and adoration for their King, lost young people are drawn to the message of salvation these songs convey.

An example of such a song is "Here I Am" written by Kate Spence[10]. I believe the words of this song truly encapsulate young people's desire to worship God:

This is perfect love you give to me
Compares to none there has ever been
How can I give back to you
All that you have given me

All you are
Is all I desire
Your gentle touch
Helps me survive
You're the air
That I breathe
Heaven's gift to me

Take my heart
Take my life
Take all I am
I give to you

Here I am
Before you I stand
No secrets to hide
I am yours
And you are mine
I'm in love.

All around the world a new sound is emerging from within the hearts of young people that is taking God's message of love, hope and salvation to the world.

You may be asking, "Where do we start? We don't have any songwriters or musicians." Don't allow a lack of resources or skill prevent you from leading your young people into worship. Use a CD player if you do not have a band. Start with what you have, and you will soon find that God will bring you the people that you need.

We must remember that worship is more than just lyrics and music.

Darlene Zschech in her book, "Extravagant Worship" succinctly captures the nature of true worship:

> "...but I have this longing in me, that the King of heaven would label me an extravagant worshipper... to worship is to be full of adoration...to bow down, to revere and to hold in awe the beauty of God. Worship is an active thing, it involves your heart, your mind, your will."

APPLICATION

As a youth leader, our priority must be to cultivate an attitude of worship in our young people. God desires more than a great band and music. He wants us to live authentic lives with hearts that earnestly seek Him.

Our role is to harness the power of music for the glory of God. Our youth ministries will only experience 'true worship' when we are first worshippers.

DNA OF A YOUTH LEADER:

Builds Healthy Relationships

"Christianity is a social religion. To turn it into a solitary religion is indeed to destroy it."

John Wesley

"Loneliness is the greatest disease of humanity."

Mother Teresa

christine caine

DNA OF A YOUTH LEADER:
Builds Healthy Relationships

A few years ago I was speaking with one of my friends; one of the most committed, faithful and gifted youth pastors I knew.

She was obviously exhausted. She had maintained an extremely full schedule over many months and not only did she need a vacation, but felt like giving up.

She had spent years pouring into the lives of young people, always on call to respond to other people's seemingly urgent problems and needs. Her life was consumed by relationships that drained her. This made her ineffective, as she had nothing left to give. She ran the risk of ministering from a place of brokenness, as she was not healthy emotionally or relationally.

If our desire is to help people over the long term, it is essential that we have relationships that replenish us, not just relationships where we are replenishing others.

ISOLATION

> "A man who isolates himself seeks his own desire; He rages against all wise judgment." (Proverbs 18:1)

It can sometimes be easy for youth leaders to become isolated. The nature of youth work is that when most people your own age are socializing you are running your youth ministry. Special effort is required to stay connected with friends.

The risk is that we can become so consumed with the work of the ministry that we go for weeks without having a night off or having gone out with people our own age. Our life can become filled with teenagers and their activities and schedules.

When I first started working with youth, it was easy to be friends with young people because I was almost their age. Now a mum in my mid-thirties, my world is very different to that of the average 14 year old. My tastes are definitely different, as is my fashion sense!

We need to take time out to interact with adults who are not involved in our youth ministry. We must never allow our world to become so insular that we risk losing the very relationships that will help replenish, build and challenge us.

In his book, "Fit to be Tied", Bill Hybels speaks of three types of relationships that we all need to have in our lives:

1. Draining Relationships

These are people who only take from us. When we have been with them we feel depleted as we are always giving.

2. Neutral Relationships

These are people that neither take from us nor give to us.

3. Replenishing Relationships

These are people who give back to us as we give to them.

We all need to ensure that we have a balance of these three relationship types in our life if we are to avoid burn out.

There are many well-meaning ex-youth leaders walking around disillusioned, burnt out and feeling used and abused because they gave the best years of their life to the youth ministry. They become bitter towards the church and ministry and feel as though it was all give and no take. I know others who feel that they have missed out on a marriage partner or have no friends because they gave all they had to the youth ministry.

It is our responsibility to build healthy relationships to ensure we do not end up hurt, angry and resentful toward God about the years we have served in ministry.

When we keep the big picture before us and stay committed to ministry for the long haul, we will take the time out from our busy schedules to build lasting relationships.

CREATED FOR RELATIONSHIP

The essence of the Gospel is about relationship. Jesus came to restore our relationship with God. He did not do this from afar, but came to earth and became involved in people's lives.

God created us for relationship, for friendship and for companionship with both God and man.

> God's first recorded statement about man was, "It is not good for the man to be alone." (Genesis 2:18)

We all have an innate need for God and other people, but sin estranged us from both. Therefore, it is not surprising that we often struggle with our relationships.

The world is full of lonely people, including many Christians. In fact, some social commentators have called loneliness the most pervasive and important problem facing society today.

American novelist Thomas Wolfe put it this way:

> *"The whole conviction of my life now rests upon the belief that loneliness, far from being a rare and curious phenomenon, peculiar to myself and a few other solitary men, is the central and inevitable fact of human existence."*

Our youth ministries have the capacity to become incubators that develop young people who will be capable of developing healthy and lasting relationships as adults. They will not suffer from loneliness because they have learnt the importance of having a variety of relationships and have discovered how to maintain a healthy balance.

Again, this starts with you the leader. I encourage you to analyze the relationships in your life. You may know many people, but how well do you really know them? Is there a depth in your relationships and is there a level of accountability in at least some of your relationships? Do you have friendships with a cross-section of age groups?

The most effective tool in teaching young people about healthy relationships is modelling these to them. Young people need to see us building great same-sex and opposite sex relationships. They need to see our marriages and families flourish.

BOUNDARIES

I have met 33 year old youth pastors who have been unable to hold their marriages together and have few, if any, friends their own age. They have gone on to develop unhealthy co-dependent relationships with teenagers in an effort to meet their own emotional needs.

They have failed to establish healthy boundaries for their relationships with the young people in their ministry and have found themselves in situations that ultimately hurt them and their young people.

It is through developing right relationships with our young people that we as leaders gain access to their lives and are able to teach them to walk in God's ways.

You may be asking, "What does a healthy boundary look like?" This depends on you. You need to be guided by God's Word and discover which boundaries are appropriate and necessary in your life. For example, if one of your youth is ringing you at home after hours every night, this is an overstepping of an appropriate boundary.

GOD'S BLUEPRINT FOR RELATIONSHIPS

In John 15:12-17, Jesus highlights five characteristics of Godly relationships as He describes His relationship with us. We should strive for these same qualities in our relationship with others:

1. The Extent of God's Friendship is Sacrificial Love

"Greater love has no one than this, than to lay down one's life for His friends." (John 15:13)

In the same way that Jesus gave His life for us, we need to lay down our life for our friends. We need to make time for our relationships and be there when they need us, even if sometimes we do not feel like it!

A relationship is not all about having our needs met, but about a mutual investment of time, energy and resources.

2. The Effect of God's Friendship is Change

"You are My friends if you do whatever I command you." (John 15:14)

Our relationships should transform and change us into better people. They should not become stagnant but help us become more Christlike.

If you have relationships that have plateaued and are perhaps even regressing, I encourage you to seek God on whether this is a relationship He wants you to maintain.

I do not keep contact with every friend I went to school or college with, as I know that some relationships were for a particular time or season. We should not allow the relationships we have outgrown prevent us from developing and changing.

3. The Expression of God's Friendship is Intimacy

"No longer do I call you servants, for a servant does not know what his master is doing; but I have called you friends for all the things I have heard from My Father I have made known to you." (John 15:15)

Christ's sacrifice on the cross was about bridging the gap between God and man. His desire is to be intimate with us. He calls us His sons and daughters, He knows everyone one of our thoughts and desires.

In the natural, we need to ensure that we have relationships where we can share our deepest struggles, vulnerabilities, challenges and temptations in a safe way. We need to carefully choose who we allow into our lives on this level, but this kind of intimacy is essential.

Without these types of relationships, we risk developing the habit of wearing masks and never really allowing God to reveal areas of weakness, wrong attitudes and mindsets in us.

Intimate relationships will help refine and mould us into the best that God has created us to be.

4. An Initiative of God's Friendship is Love

"You did not choose me, but I chose you..." (John 15:16)

I am amazed by the fact that God loved us while we were yet sinners. He sent His Son to earth all too aware of our imperfections, and He saved us by grace.

Similarly, our friendships should be built on love. If we waited for perfection before we loved, we would be waiting a long time! We need to accept one another despite our imperfections. However, we need to be committed to inspiring each other to greater levels.

5. The Goal Of God's Friendship Is Fruitfulness

> "...You should go and bear fruit, and that your fruit should remain." (John 15:16)

Just as the quality of fruit denotes the health of a tree, the fruit of our relationships determines their health.

The Fruits of the Spirit: love, peace, joy, longsuffering, kindness, goodness, faithfulness and self-control should be evident in all our relationships. It is this fruit that will ensure that our friendships last.

If our relationships are bearing anger, jealousy, insecurity, doubt and negativity, I would suggest it is time to take stock of these and assess where they are heading.

I have found the following penetrating questions very useful when evaluating my relationships with others:

- What are the limits of my friendship? Do I use people or lay down my life for them?
- What is my impact on others? Are my friends better disciples of Christ because of me?
- Am I vulnerable with my friends? Do I establish

impenetrable walls around my life?
- Do I verbally express my love and appreciation of my friends?
- Do I choose people as friends because of my needs or their needs?
- Am I helping my friends realize their potential in life?

APPLICATION

Biblical friendships are not based on our need for others but their need for us. There is risk and cost involved in building these kinds of relationships, but the prize is worth the price.

Godly relationships will help grow, replenish and fuel you. They will undoubtedly impact the lives of your young people as you model and teach them how to build and maintain healthy relationships.

christine caine

DNA OF A YOUTH LEADER:

Lives Generously

"Giving is being a Christian."

Dr Phil Pringle

christine caine

DNA OF A YOUTH LEADER:
Lives Generously

The atmosphere was amazing. There was such a sense of expectancy. For more than an hour, young people had been bringing their offerings to the Lord. It was the first time anything like this had happened in Norway.

We had prayed, prepared and believed God that something significant was going to take place as young people gave.

People have often told me not to expect too much from young people, as they do not give. I have never held this view as I know better than to underestimate God.

In the year 2000, I began to notice a shift in the level of young people's giving. Wherever I went, it seemed young people were outgiving adults (these offerings were never received for me personally but for the ministries I was with). Something had changed in young people's attitudes toward giving.

I had been in a meeting in Australia where 420 young people gave over $25,000 cash. In California, 320 young people gave more than $15,000, and we had seen supernatural offerings in our state youth rallies that were full of unbelievers (now that is a miracle)!

Therefore, I was filled with faith and expecting God to do something awesome in Norway. Before this offering, the biggest had been 40,000 Kroner (AUS$10,000). Yet Nick and I believed we would see these same young people give 250,000 Kroner (AUS$62,500). I dared not share this figure with the leaders, as they would have thought we were insane!

We continued to worship for hours that night and the presence of God was so evident. Young people were dealing with issues before God and pledging to lay down their life for the cause of the Gospel. I ensured that there was no confusion in the translation of the message, as I wanted no one to think they were being manipulated to give. When the offering was finally counted, 269,000 Kroner (AUS$67,250) had been given. The crowd exploded into spontaneous applause, shouting cheering and thanking God.

Some of you may be thinking, "It was a one off. The young people were hyped up because of the atmosphere." The truth is, in Norway and many of the other places where we had witnessed phenomenal offerings, the young people's level of giving continued to increase after the event. This tells me that something significant happened in the hearts of those young people.

On every occasion that I have seen a miracle offerings given, young people were hungry to see a breakthrough in their youth ministry and communities. They wanted to see their youth pastors paid, facilities hired and outreach programs move ahead. They were prepared to give by faith, and this produced extraordinary results.

I have included these testimonies of supernatural giving purely to help inspire you and to lift your expecations of what is possible with faith and vision.

RESOURCING THE KINGDOM

I know some of you must be struggling with this whole concept of giving, prosperity and generosity. Your young people barely attend youth let alone give money to help fund the youth ministry. Others struggle week to week with fundraisers, car washes and chocolate drives. Still others think, "My kids really do not have that sort of money", or, "youth ministry is not about money it is about people".

I agree, youth ministry is about people, but we need money to help reach young people.

In Australia, the teenage market is worth billions of dollars to advertisers. Coca-Cola, McDonalds, Billabong and the music industry know that young people have money, and they spend a lot of time and resource convincing this generation to buy their products.

Advertisers know that young people are willing to pay for something they want or value. The question we need to ask ourselves is, "What value do my young people put on the youth ministry?"

I guarantee that once young people grasp the eternal value of what your church is doing, they will be less likely to spend the $10 in their wallet on candy and Coke, and be willing to invest it to see their friends reached and transformed by the Gospel. Young people will be enthusiastic about giving their time, money and resources if they know a cause is changing the world. Young people give to vision.

ARE YOU A GIVER?

Some leaders struggle with the principle of tithing, and predictably, so do their young people. Tithing is not a suggestion. Malachi 3:8-9 makes this point clear:

> "Will a man rob God? Yet you have robbed Me! But you say, 'In what way have we robbed You?' In tithes and offerings. You are cursed with a curse for you have robbed Me."

Tithing ensures God's blessing in our life and His protection over us and all that we do (Malachi 3:10-11). It also guarantees that the church will have enough to fulfil its ministries.

If we as leaders are not tithing then our young people are not likely to tithe, nor will they be inclined to give offerings.

It is important that we have a revelation of the power of tithing so we can confidently teach this principle to our young people.

We owe it to a generation to teach them the Biblical principles of sowing and reaping, putting the house of God first, and training young people to be wise stewards of their money. Biblical economics will ensure that they have blessed and prosperous lives.

Just as schools have no problem teaching economics from a worldly perspective, we should be proactively advocating God's financial plan for success to our young people.

CULTIVATING GENEROSITY

Generosity is more than a willingness to give of our finance. We can be generous with our words, our actions and with our time. Generosity should be a way of life.

If we are going to build youth ministries that are generous, then we as youth leaders must cultivate a lifestyle of generosity.

The following principles will help you cultivate generosity in yourself and your young people:

1. The Exit From Need is Always Seed

We often think we have nothing to give to God. We look at life from a perspective of what we do not have as opposed to what we DO have. We look at our limitations and not our assets.

I have encountered many youth leaders who have an impoverished mentality when it comes to ministry. They have a 'barely get by' attitude and seem trapped in a cycle of financial struggle.

I am aware that there is always more vision than money, but this should not stop us from pressing in and sowing seed. We need to believe God for increase.

I love the story in Luke 21:1-4 of the widow who gave the two mites. Although she did not have much, she was willing to give all she had.

God does not want us bound by a poverty mentality. His resources are endless, but we tap into His provision by giving.

Tithing is not a debt 'we owe' but a seed 'we sow'. The exit from our place of need is always seed. If we want a prosperous youth ministry, we must first sow seed.

1 Kings 17:8–16 tells us the story of Elijah and the widow. She was focused on what she did not have rather than what she did have. She could not conceive of giving the prophet the small amount of flour and oil she believed was going to be her last supper before she died. Elijah had a different perspective; he saw these as the very seeds necessary for a miracle.

When she finally relented and gave her last crumbs away, she got her miracle; the oil and flour did not run out.

Giving sets in motion the eternal principle of sowing and reaping. Withholding and containing resource will eventually lead to our resources drying up. If we want our lives to flourish and our youth ministries to move up to a new level then we must be willing to sow seed.

2. Sowing and Reaping an Eternal Law Not Just a Good Idea

> *"Do not be deceived, God is not mocked; for whatever a man sows, that he will also reap."* (Galatians 6:7)

Every farmer knows that to reap a crop or harvest you must first sow seed. In the natural, you cannot sow orange seeds and expect to reap a harvest of apples. Similarly, in the spiritual, you must first sow what it is you want and you will reap accordingly.

The Bible teaches us that God so loved the world that He gave His only son (John 3:16). When God wanted to restore a lost humanity to Himself, He sowed His own flesh and blood - Jesus. Essentially, God sowed a life to reap humanity.

If you want to reap finances then you have to sow finances. If you want a youth ministry that speaks generous words, then you must begin sowing generous words.

Take your focus off what your young people or the church are not doing, and instead consider sowing some seed in these areas to activate the eternal principle of sowing and reaping. Then ensure you water that seed with God's Word and prayer, and you will reap a mighty harvest.

3. Generosity Releases God's Provision

The Bible clearly teaches in Proverbs 11:24-25, *"There is one who scatters, yet increases more; and there is one who withholds more than is right, but it leads to poverty. The generous soul will be made rich, and he who waters will also be watered himself."*

Holding onto the things that God has asked us to give can be likened to a kink in a garden hose. It stops the flow of God's provision into our life. We need to listen to God and learn to trust Him to provide for us.

Our world is consumed with the attitude of, 'get all you can and hold onto it'. The Kingdom of God operates in the totally opposite way. God's way is 'the more we give the more we will receive'. As a youth leader, are you cultivating a lifestyle of giving?

4. Prosperity is Biblical

God's desire is that His people prosper. *"Let the Lord be magnified, who has pleasure in the prosperity of His servant."* (Psalm 35:27).

God wants every aspect of our lives to be blessed and prosperous, including our health, relationships, spiritual life and finances.

Religious thinking and tradition about prosperity has kept many leaders in bondage. Some feel that Christian leaders who speak about money and prosperity are carnal or materialistic. The truth is that money can accomplish much for the Kingdom of God. We need finances to run effective youth ministries.

Real blessing is not about what someone can give to us, but what we are able to give to others. Our youth ministries exist to serve the young people of our communities. To effectively do this, we need to have resource so we can give resource.

God wants our lives, friendships, families and ministries to be blessed in every way. Therefore, our thinking must be renewed to allow us to begin to live according to the Biblical pattern of prosperity.

APPLICATION

Generosity releases God's provision and blessing in our life and, in turn, the lives of our young people. It is more than how much money we have, it is a way of life. When we choose to be generous in every thought, word and deed and begin to sow this into the lives of others, we are sure to reap the benefits in our ministries and see generosity reproduced in our young people.

DNA OF A YOUTH LEADER:

Builds Lives

"To live a worthwhile, meaningful life, a person must be part of building something greater than themselves."

Anonymous

"Unless the Lord builds the house, They labor in vain who build it."

(Psalm 127:1)

christine caine

DNA OF A YOUTH LEADER:
Builds Lives

Just as a house is built one brick at a time, a youth ministry is built one life at a time. Youth leaders need to have passion, vision and commitment to building their life and the lives of their young people.

In the natural, builders plan before they build; they have a blueprint to work from and they realize there is always a cost involved, and time required when building. Most of all, they recognize that the building's foundation is pivotal to the success of the project.

Equally so, the foundation on which we build will determine whether our youth ministries will produce fruit that will last.

In the parable of the wise and foolish builders, Jesus explains the implications of building a foundation on any other than Him:

> "I will show you what he is like who comes to me and hears my word and puts them into practice. He is like a man building a house, who dug down deep and laid the foundation on rock. When a flood came, the torrent struck that house but could not shake it, because it was well built. But the one that hears my words and does not put them in practice is like a man who built a house on the ground without a foundation. The moment the torrent struck that house, it collapsed and its destruction was complete."
> (Luke 6:47-49)

When we build our lives and ministries on Jesus, we will withstand the storms and challenges that will invaribly come.

Similarly, when we teach our young people to build their lives on the Rock, they will stand firm and live lives that are committed to Christ.

PRINCIPLES OF BUILDING

We can learn from the principles implemented by Nehemiah, one of history's greatest builders, and apply them to our life and youth ministry.

Nehemiah started life as a cupbearer in the Persian King's court and ended up rebuilding the broken walls of Jerusalem. He had a vision to restore the Jewish city, driving him to complete a 52 day miracle.

Like Nehemiah, we are surrounded by the brokenness – the fragmented lives of young people. God has given us the awesome privilege of rebuilding those lives and mobilizing them for mission. If we want to see miracles in our youth ministries, we need to have the single-minded focus of Nehemiah. We must be prepared for the challenges of building something that will outlive us.

THINGS TO EXPECT WHEN BUILDING

We can ensure that we are successful builders by expecting and being prepared for the following:

1. Opposition

> *"When Sanballat the Horonite and Tobiah the Ammonite official heard of it, they were deeply disturbed that a man had come to seek the well-being of the children of Israel...But it so happened, when Sanballat heard that we were rebuilding the wall, that he was furious and very indignant and mocked the Jews."*
> (Nehemiah 2:10 & 4:1)

Even the mention of someone asking about the welfare of the Israelites caused concern among Israel's enemies. As long as the Israelites were separated and defeated they were little threat. In the same way, the enemy gets nervous when you get serious about building your youth ministry.

Events and activities that are not purpose-driven do not get the devil's attention. It is when we are filled with vision and fuelled by passion about seeing lives transformed that the enemy will launch His attack.

We do not need to overemphasize the devil as we have the greater power through Christ. However, it is important that we are not ignorant of his devices. We are in a spiritual battle - we are fighting for the eternal lives of young people.

> *"For we do not wrestle against flesh and blood, but against principalities, against powers, against the rulers of darkness of this age, against spiritual hosts of wickedness in the heavenly places."* (Ephesians 6:12)

It is not just the devil that is opposed to us; be prepared for the fact that people in your community (perhaps even other Christians!) will become distressed that you want to build a good work.

When I decided to enter full time youth ministry, my family was devastated. They thought I was throwing away my life, education, marriage prospects and financial future. I remember many tearful exchanges whilst trying to explain why I had made the decision. I could not understand why the fact that I wanted to help people would so upset them. One of the members of my family said to me, "When you were going out to nightclubs and dating lots of people, at least that was normal." Normality was equated with living for the moment and without purpose.

I know my choices challenged my family's thinking. Their only point of reference for full time ministry were the nuns and priests from the Orthodox Church we attended. My decision to go to Bible College and my commitment to full-time ministry was outside of their worldview. They had my best interests at heart, but they could not comprehend my decision.

Like Nehemiah, we all have a choice to make; will we allow opposition to keep us from building the thing that God has purposed, in favor of keeping the status-quo? Be prepared for opposition.

2. Ridicule

> "But when Sanballat the Horonite, Tobiah the Ammonite official, and Geshem the Arab heard of it [the rebuilding], they laughed at us and despised us, and said, "What is this thing you are doing?" (Nehemiah 2:19)

I have lost count of the number of times I have heard someone say to me, "Who do you think you are?" or "What difference do you think you are really going to make?"

Nehemiah's opponents ridiculed him even before the first brick was replaced. They could not believe that one man could rally disenchanted people to a cause greater than themselves.

In the same way, when you dare to live the vision for your youth ministry you will have ridicule hurled at you. Our vision and dreams can often seem ridiculous to others. But remember, they cannot see what you see.

Negative, critical and hurtful things may be said and people may try to convince you why it cannot be done, criticizing your abilities and motives.

If you are going to finish whatever God has put in your heart to build, you will need to learn to deflect these comments. Let God, your deep conviction and determination fuel you.

3. Fear

> *"And our adversaries said, "They will neither know nor see anything, till we come into their midst and kill them and cause the work to cease. So it was, when the Jews who dwelt near them came, they told us ten times, "From whatever place you turn, they will be upon us." (Nehemiah 4:11-12)*

Nehemiah did not let the opposition and the ridicule take his focus from rebuilding the wall. As the work was progressing and the gaps were closing, the enemy decided to attack Jerusalem. They tried to instil fear and cause confusion among the laborers.

Nehemiah made a choice to keep pressing on towards the goal and not bow down to fear. In the face of the enemy he focused on God rather than fear and he rallied the workers.

> *"Do not be afraid of them. Remember the Lord, great and awesome, and fight for your brethren, your sons, your daughters, your wives, and your houses."* (Nehemiah 4:14)

As you choose to build a youth ministry, the enemy will try to cripple you by fear. He will begin to attack your thoughts. He will try to convince you that you cannot do what you have set out to do. He will speak to your weakness and sow seeds of doubt.

A study by the University if Michigan found that 95 per cent of all fear is unfounded. That is, fear is false evidence appearing real. It is predominantly a battle of the mind.

Psychiatrist Victor Frankl said: *"Fear makes come true that which one is afraid of."*

When we focus on our fear, it is extremely difficult to continue being effective.

What I love about the story of Nehemiah is that although his enemies were very real, he did not focus all his resources and energy on fighting them. He prepared half of his men for the battle while the other half continued building (Nehemiah 4:16).

We must walk in the knowledge that God has given us a wall to rebuild. Do not allow fear to rob you of it.

"God has not given us a spirit of fear but of love, power and a sound mind." (2 Timothy 2:17)

4. False Accusations

"Then Sanballat sent his servant to me as before, the fifth time, with an open letter in his hand. In it was written: It is reported among the nations and Geshem says, that you and the Jews plan to rebel; therefore, according to those rumors, you are rebuilding the wall, that you may be their king." (Nehemiah 6:5-6)

As Nehemiah continued to lead the rebuilding of the walls, the officials deliberately tried to harm his reputation by falsely accusing him.

Jesus, although perfect, was falsely accused. It was these accusations that sent Him to the cross.

We must understand that false accusations will come as we build God's plans and purposes on the earth. If we stay focused on Jesus, and do not lose heart, we will accomplish that which He created us to do.

APPLICATION

We need to commit to building the lives of our young people and the best way to do this is by making Jesus the foundation of their lives. As in any building endeavor there will always be obstacles, hurdles and challenges to overcome. It will also involve much hard work and perseverance. Remember, the end result is always worth it.

christine caine

DNA OF A YOUTH LEADER:

A Team Player

"You can do what I cannot do. I can do what you cannot do. Together we can do great things."

Mother Teresa

christine caine

DNA OF A YOUTH LEADER:
A Team Player

"I can't do this anymore, Chris, it is just too hard. I am burnt out, tired, angry and disappointed. This did not turn out how I expected." I was sitting in the snow, outside the meeting hall at a youth camp in California, consoling yet another disillusioned youth pastor. She had come to the end of the road and could not face going inside to host another camp meeting.

After several hours of talking and crying, I realized that Susan's* problem was not about the youth, or a lack of passion, but the fact that for the past year she had tried to do everything herself.

She coordinated the meetings, the follow-up, the Bible studies and the social events. She tried to be there for all of the young people and their families.

Predictably, the pressure and workload became unbearable and she could not take it any more. She could have become another statistic, another youth pastor who left the ministry, tired and burnt out.

Instead, we started a mentoring program and I helped her to develop a team around her to assist her with he work of the ministry.

WE ARE NOT CALLED TO DO IT ALONE

We were not designed by God to do ministry or carry the burden alone. Think of any significant achievement and I guarantee a team was involved.

If you want longevity in youth ministry, build a team or join a team. An effective youth leader must be a great team builder and team player. If we build a team, and then participate in that team, we are more likely to last the distance in youth ministry. There is always too much work to be done for any one person; building a team will maximize a leader's potential as teams can always do more than an individual.

Jesus knew the power of team, *"And He called the twelve to Himself, and began to send them out two by two, and gave them power over unclean spirits."* (Mark 6:7)

In his book, "Developing the Leaders Around You", John Maxwell uses the example of horses to illustrate the importance of teams:

> "At a Midwestern fair, many spectators gathered for an old fashioned horse pull (an event where various weights are put on a horse-drawn sled and pulled along the ground). The grand champion horse pulled a sled with 4,500 pounds on it. The runner-up was close, with a 4,440-pound pull. Some of the men wondered what the two horses could pull if hitched together. Separately they totalled nearly 9,000 pounds, but when hitched and working together as a team, they pulled over 12,000 pounds."

We cannot multiply time but we can multiply people. The only way we can do all that needs to be done, is to adopt Jesus' method of leadership. He poured His life into 12 other leaders. He trained, empowered and equipped them, and they in turn did that with others. Consequently, the whole world is being impacted with the Gospel of Jesus Christ.

TEAMS ARE AN INVESTMENT

When I was developing a new strategy for Youth Alive NSW, I knew that I could not physically care for every youth ministry in my State. I built a team of 12 regional leaders, who were responsible for building teams in their regions, and together, we covered the entire state.

I believe that the degree to which you build a team will be the level to which you will build a significant youth ministry. You must lay down your ego and insecurity to attract great and strong people around you. If you help others maximize their potential and fulfil their dream, you will fulfil yours.

A wise youth leader will invest into relationships with potential leaders who will build relationships directly with young people.

A BIG VISION

In order to attract leaders, I had to have a vision big enough to involve them, a vision that would release them into their God given destiny. I also had to be committed to serve them and nurture their growth. My time was spent investing into them, which they in turn did with their youth leaders. Subsequently, our programs grew and became more effective because we all shared the load.

If I had tried to do it all alone, I would have grown weary and would never have completed the job. As a team, we carried the load together, shared the victories and disappointments, encouraged and supported each other. We became genuine friends because we were all laying down our life for the same cause. I did not feel isolated, used, or overburdened, and I was released to lead, spread the vision and concentrate on my strengths while others flourished in theirs.

I had to trust people with the vision and empower them to act. There were times when people did not follow through or keep their commitment, but there are always risks involved in being a part of a team. After all it was Judas, one of Jesus' team, who betrayed Him. However, the benefits of a team always outweigh the risks. When you communicate the vision and allow your team members to own it and be part of the process in seeing it fulfilled, great power is unleashed. Your ministry begins to operate as a body and each member is released to do its part.

SURROUND YOURSELF WITH GREAT PEOPLE

We can sometimes feel intimidated by people who are more gifted or talented than we are in a certain area. These are the very people we need to surround ourselves with. It takes a big person to surround themselves with great people. A wise youth leader will always ensure that they have these kinds of people on their team.

None of us has every gift or every skill necessary to successfully grow a youth ministry. 1 Corinthians 12:18- 21 makes this clear:

> "But now God has set the members, each one of them, in the body just as He pleased. And if they were all one member, where would the body be? But now indeed there are many members, yet one body. And the eye cannot say to the hand, 'I have no need for you'; nor again the head to the feet, 'I have no need for you."

I marvel at the leadership of my pastors Brian and Bobbie Houston, who surround themselves with great people who love God. They openly promote, encourage and inspire our team to go to new levels.

We too must be committed to helping people fulfil their dreams, and not just use young people to fulfil our own dream. Using your young people to build your team is not the goal. The team exists to build your young people.

STEPS TO TEAM BUILDING

1. Have a vision big enough and worthwhile enough for others to follow
2. Develop an ability to communicate the vision with passion and clarity
3. Genuinely care for your leaders personally
4. Clearly assign responsibilities to your youth leaders
5. Teach, train and equip your leaders to fulfil their responsibilities
6. Ensure the right people are in the right position
7. Release and empower leaders to fulfil their mandate
8. Give leaders permission to fail and learn from their mistakes
9. Celebrate successes together
10. Support one another at all times
11. Have fun together

APPLICATION

Build a team who desires to do whatever it takes to fulfil the vision, and who are committed to you as a leader. Actively invest into the lives of your team members, help them discover their gifts and strengths and start to release them in these areas. You will be amazed at what God will do through a united and healthy team who are working together to see God's purposes fulfilled.

DNA OF A YOUTH LEADER:

A Mobilizer Of Young People

"Do not say, I am a youth, For you shall go to all to whom I send you, and whatever I command you, you shall speak."

(Jeremiah 1:7)

"Let no one despise your youth, but be an example to the believers in word, conduct, in love, in spirit in faith, in purity."

(1 Timothy 4:12)

christine caine

DNA OF A YOUTH LEADER:
A Mobilizer Of Young People

Eldrick (Tiger) Woods has had an unprecedented career since becoming a professional golfer in 1996, at the age of 20. Tiger played in his first professional tournament in 1992, at age 16.

He has won 40 tournaments, 29 of those on the PGA TOUR. With his second Masters victory in 2001, Tiger became the first ever to hold all four professional major championships at the same time.

On June 15, 1997, in his 42nd week as a professional, Woods became the youngest ever No. 1 golfer at age 21 years, 24 weeks. He achieved No. 1 on the Official World Golf Ranking for the most rapid progression ever to that position. Tiger Woods had won US$32,795,974 worldwide up to the end of 2001[11].

Similarly, Australian swimmer Ian Thorpe won several Olympic gold medals and broke world records while still a teenager.

Obviously, Tiger Woods and Ian Thorpe did not allow their age to prevent them from achieving great success in their chosen sport. Similarly, as leaders, we should see age as an opportunity, not a barrier.

We should resist shying away from releasing young people to reach young people. They possess an energy, passion, ideas and creativity which is unrivalled. Our role is to help mobilize and release them into their God given potential.

GIVE THEM A GO

I am amazed that teenagers can win international tennis titles, golf titles and Olympic gold medals but some church leaders remain hesitant to release them in areas of church service and leadership.

My pastor has often said that as we get older, we become more resistant to trusting the next generation, and less willing to take risks on them. We may think they are not mature or experienced enough to handle the responsibility.

Garth Herichs puts it this way: *"In youth we want to change the world. In old age we want to change youth."*

Who of us can honestly say that we were fully confident of our ability when offered a new role or responsibility? Whenever we take on a new challenge, it is always bigger than us. We trust God to help us enlarge.

Of course, it is important to determine appropriate levels and boundaries in which students can lead and serve in ministry. I believe we should exercise wisdom before promotion, but I know the most effective way to reach young people is by mobilizing young people to the cause of Christ.

As the Director of Youth Alive, I always ensured that young people were an integral part of our ministry. The band included a 14 year old bass guitarist who played in front of 11,000 people, 16 year old songwriters who penned songs that are now sung around the world, teenagers who have put together drama and video presentations which were played to packed stadiums and young people who volunteered their time to willingly phone literally hundreds of youth leaders about our upcoming events.

The Bible is full of young people who have made a difference in their world. Daniel, Caleb, Esther, Jeremiah and the disciples were all young. God has, and continues to use young people to achieve His purposes and plans.

Young people need to feel important, to make a difference, to feel useful, to be part of something worthwhile. If we are committed to training and equipping our young people for a spiritual battle, we need to let them walk onto the battlefield.

THEY ARE INFLUENCERS

It was one of the most memorable events of the late 20th century. With China seemingly on the verge of a new era, students occupied Tiananmen Square in Beijing to demand democratic reforms. Suddenly, the protestors found themselves facing tanks. On June 3 and 4 1989, the People's Liberation Army brutally crushed pro-democracy supporters, killing hundreds and injuring 10,000 others. The extremely violent suppression of the Tiananmen Square protest caused widespread international condemnation of the Chinese government.

Similarly, in the 1960s and early 1970s, it was college students who protested against the United States' involvement in the Vietnam War on college campuses across America.

Lenin, the mastermind behind communist Russia, also recognized the power of youth in implementing change and influencing culture. In a speech he delivered to the Third All-Russian Congress of the Russian Young Communist League in 1920[12], he said:

> *"Only by radically remolding the teaching, organization and training of the youth shall we be able to ensure the efforts of the younger generation will result in the creation of a society that will be unlike the old society, i.e., in the creation of a communist society."*

Young people have the power and ability to influence not only their generation, but also their world.

A 15 year old student has more influence with their friends than we do. You may see them once a week at your youth meeting, but their friends are with them almost daily. We need to trust our young people to run Bible studies, prayer meetings and to organize events to reach the young people in their sphere of influence.

Their high school or college is their mission field. Christian students are on campus five days a week living the Christian life for all to see. As leaders, our goal should be to inspire our young people to develop God's compassion for their lost friends and to accept the responsibility of sharing Christ with them.

THERE ARE RISKS

You may be thinking, "I've tried to mobilize my youth, but they have always let me down." There are risks in mobilizing your young people for a cause. They may forget to turn up, not follow through, or totally overlook what you have asked them to do.

It will take time, patience, and the ability to exercise forgiveness. Perhaps it will mean sacrificing a level of professionalism or excellence for a season as you build and train them.

It may seem a whole lot quicker and simpler to do it yourself, (it often is) but over the long term, many more people will be released into ministry, and subsequently more people will be reached.

Your decision to mobilize young people will create a youth ministry that is not just about attendance, but involvement. It does not only release young people into their area of gifting or passion, it will also develop young leaders around you who will help release you as they take on some of the load.

RELEASING VISION

Ensure that your vision team is not exclusively made up of people who no longer constitute your target market. Young people will bring creative, vibrant, relevant ideas, (perhaps, not always practical) because they know young people- after all, they are one. Of course, a leader is there to give overall direction (they are the one hearing from God and prophetically taking the youth ministry into the future) but if we release young people, we will see incredible fruit.

APPLICATION

If you are prepared to take some risks and encounter some disappointments, expect to see amazing miracles come to pass in and through your young people.

We sometimes earnestly pray that God will send us laborers to help us with the harvest. Who has He already given you? They may not always look the part of a leader, but it is our mission to help them become all that God has destined them to be.

christine caine

youth ministry

DNA OF A YOUTH LEADER:

A Committment To Discipleship

"He who spends the most time wins."

Jeanne Mayo

christine caine

DNA OF A YOUTH LEADER:
A Committment To Discipleship

I wept as I watched 1076 young people walk from the front of the stage to the counselling room. This event, held at the Sydney Entertainment Centre, was my final rally as Youth Alive Director. I knew the Holy Spirit was drawing young people to Jesus and when I gave the invitation for them to receive Christ as their personal Lord and Savior, the aisles filled.

My elation was not due to the fact that people had come forward. For years people have been responding to altar calls in stadiums all over the world. The reason for my excitement was that I knew the rally was filled with unchurched students who had been invited by friends. These friends were already part of dynamic youth ministries from across our state. I knew that those students who made a decision that night already had a connection with a vibrant youth group and a friend to walk alongside them. This is where discipleship would begin.

DISCIPLES NOT DECISIONS

> "Go therefore and make disciples of all the nations..."
> (Matthew 28:19)

If every Christian were to win one person to Christ each year, then train that person to do the same, we could win the world for Christ in just 32 years. Now that is multiplication and effectiveness!

I do not believe that God wants us to host evangelistic rallies and ask people to respond to the Gospel, but then not give them any real direction on what to do next or how to get connected with a church.

I have met youth leaders who believe youth ministry is all about numbers, a crowd and decisions.

I understand that a tangible measure for growth is the number of people you have attending your youth service or how many decisions you have each week, but youth ministry is much more than this.

The real question is where will those young people be in five to ten years time?

When a young person moves on from our youth ministry, we need to ask ourselves, "How effectively have we reproduced ourselves in the lives of our students and nurtured their personal walk with Christ?"

Seeing the growth in your young people is not always immediately evident as making disciples takes time.

I encourage you not to fall into the trap of chasing decisions instead of making disciples.

An event or program has its place, but the real work of the ministry happens daily. This is not normally glamorous, but can be quite thankless and often exhausting. There are usually no spotlights, acknowledgements or applause. However, there is God who looks down and is well pleased with those who take on the daily task of turning unchurched young people into disciplined followers of Jesus Christ.

IT'S PERSONAL

Discipleship takes Christianity from a weekly event to a daily pilgrimage. It means that we must allow young people access to our lives as discipleship infers proximity. People have to get close enough to our lives to allow us to pour into theirs.

It is not about information dissemination, but rather impartation that results in life transformation.

Your young people need to see how you deal with stress, temptation, crisis, disappointment, success and the challenges of life. Scary? This is where real growth and change occurs.

Remember, your young people do not expect you to be perfect. They would much prefer that you are real and honest about your struggles and mistakes. They want to know that you are giving it your best, and like them, you face challenges too.

IT TAKES TIME

Young people equate time with love. If you keep the purpose and the goal before you, you will not despise the process of discipleship. Our role as leaders is to help young people grow in their personal day-to-day relationship with Jesus.

All of the hours you spend investing into the lives of young people, organizing Bible studies, camps, picking them up or just hanging out with them, is the process necessary for earning the right to speak into their lives.

I have discovered that real discipleship is a function that takes place between the meetings - on the way home, over a milkshake or a burger. It is not always convenient, but it is essential if we are going to help grow leaders who themselves can train and grow disciplined followers of Jesus Christ.

I once heard someone say, "Tell me and I'll forget, show me and I'll remember; walk with me and I'll understand." We need to help young people move from a Christianity they know and talk about, to a Christianity they experience.

In our 21st century world, it is often more comfortable preaching sermons or recommending books, tapes or conferences on discipleship instead of paying the price to disciple young people.

When a young person moves on from the youth ministry, rarely will they say that a particular sermon or event changed their life. They are much more likely to remember the person who was willing to pour out their life for them. Jesus did this with His disciples and He expects us to do the same.

I was mentoring a young youth pastor who was very gifted in programming and building great meetings. After a year his youth ministry had grown significantly and continued to grow each week. However, I noticed over time that there was always a new group of young people coming through the door. Many others were leaving through the 'back door'.

I realized why the 'turnover' of young people was taking place after asking him about how much time he was personally spending with young people outside of the Friday program. The answer was - none.

I also discovered that he was not effectively discipling his own leaders, who he in turn expected to disciple his young people. Your leaders will not do what you yourself are not prepared to do.

Yes, young people were attracted to a great program, but there was nothing of substance to hold them there. This soon changed, as did the youth ministry's retention rate.

I have had youth leaders say to me, "I never had anyone disciple me and I made it, why should we invest so much time, energy and resource into this generation?"

You may have made it but think how much more effective you may have been if the right tools were put in your hand earlier. We have a responsibility to train and equip the next generation.

I thank God for that 'someone' who was willing to disciple me, even when I did not look like I was going to make it, when I was rude, irrational, demanding, insecure and rebellious. Somehow they were able to see beyond all of my 'unpleasantries' to my God given destiny.

I am where I am today because they never gave up on me.

APPLICATION

There is a genuine need in youth ministry today for people who are willing to step into the life of a teenager and walk with them through the good and the challenging times, always believeing in their potential.

Discipleship is not necessarily glamorous or convenient, but it opens a doorway into the lives of our young people. It allows us to teach and train them in the ways of God. It is only through discipleship that decisions FOR Christ will become disciples OF Christ.

christine caine

SECTION THREE

Reproducing the Generations

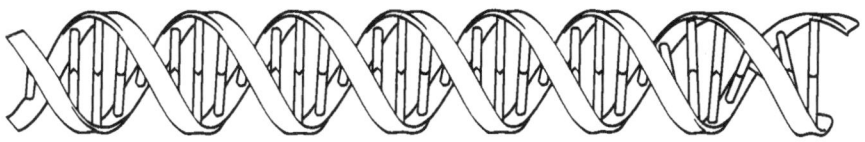

"True success comes only when every generation continues to develop the next generation."

John Maxwell

youth ministry

YOUR CHURCH -

One Generation From Extinction

"We are now living in one of the greatest periods of species extinction in the history of the planet."

Leonard Sweet

christine caine

YOUR CHURCH – One Generation From Extinction

I specifically wanted to include a chapter in this book for senior pastors, as I believe that if youth ministries are going to grow and flourish, senior leadership must be committed to facilitating ministry for young people.

Quite simply, the senior pastor's vision for the youth ministry will determine the level to which it grows. If the senior pastor has a vision for a thriving youth ministry, it will thrive. Conversely, if the senior pastor has no real vision for the youth ministry, it will be fragmented, disjointed and largely ineffective.

I can unequivocally say, if the youth pastor does not feel valued, or supported, or part of the overall vision of the church, they are more likely to seek opportunities elsewhere. Also, very little fruit will be produced through the youth ministry and few young people will stay with your church beyond adolescence.

LEAVING A LEGACY

I am aware that there are many aspects to church life, and different priorities vying for a senior pastor's time. But if we are committed to leaving a legacy that will outlive us and influence the generations to come, we must be willing to invest time, energy, and resources into youth pastors and youth ministry.

Church should be about raising and training generations of people who will be key to the ongoing work of the Lord.

Joshua's life teaches us about the importance of leaving a legacy. Although Joshua led the children of Israel into the Promised Land, he did not succeed in leaving the legacy that God required of him.

One of the saddest scriptures in the Bible refers to Joshua's death.

> "When all that generation had been gathered to their fathers, **another generation arose after them who did not know the Lord nor the work which he had done for Israel.**"
> (Judges 2:10)

What a sad thing it would be to invest a lifetime into the work of the Lord only to have everything die with you.

We all have a responsibility to leave behind some kind of legacy after we are gone. If we do not do this through the next generation, then, like Absalom, we will end up trying to do it in another way. Absalom built a monument to himself to be remembered by, as he had not reproduced any sons or daughters.

> "Now Absalom in his lifetime had taken and set up a pillar for himself in the King's Valley. For he said. '**I have no son to keep my name in remembrance.**' He called the pillar in his own name." (2 Samuel 18:18)

One of the responsibilities of a leader is to teach the generations after us the things we have learned. Psalm 78: 1- 7 exhorts us to:

> *"Incline your ears to the words of my mouth. I will open my mouth in a parable; I will utter dark sayings of old, which we have heard and known, and our fathers have told us. We will not hide them from our children, **telling the generations to come** the praises of our Lord, and His strength and His wonderful works that He has done…**that the generations to come might know them**, the children who were born, that they may arise and declare them to their children, that they may set their hope in God."*

Monuments will fade and disintegrate, memories and achievements will be forgotten. It is only through teaching, training, building and growing people that we can hope to leave a lasting legacy for the Kingdom of God.

GOD IS A GENERATIONAL GOD

It is God's will that we are fruitful in our ministries. In fact the first words spoken by God to man were:

> *"Be fruitful and multiply; fill the earth and subdue it; have dominion over the fish of the sea, over the birds of the air and over every living thing that moves on the earth."*
> (Genesis 1:28)

Multiplication and fruitfulness are in the very DNA of creation. As pastors, we should have a genuine commitment to building churches that are reproducing the generations. God is a generational

God. He is the God of Abraham, Isaac and Jacob. His covenants were made with the generations in mind. He sent His son Jesus to the earth not to save just one generation, but all people.

Everything about God is visionary and future orientated. In the same way, we should be ensuring the future of our churches by investing into young people.

Often we can look at young people as the church of the future. They will be the leaders, pastors and business people of tomorrow, but they also have so much to offer your church today.

Paul said to Timothy:

> "Let no one despise your youth, but be an example to the believers in word, in conduct, in love, in spirit, in faith, in purity." (1Timothy 4:12)

The world recognizes the abilities of young people in sports, the arts and education. The church must also empower and release young people while they are young.

In our church, my pastors are committed to raising up a generation of young people who are in love with their King, passionate about the House of God and committed to reaching the lost. Young people are involved in many aspects of church life including the ministry of helps, creative arts, hospitality, children and youth. There is nothing better than allowing young people to sow their gifts and talents into the Kingdom of God.

Young people bring an energy and exuberance to the House of God and people are attracted to it. One of the comments we often receive at Hillsong Church is about the number of awesome, cool young people who fill our services. I believe this is due to the leadership's commitment to building, investing and releasing young people.

THE YOUTH PASTOR AS AN ALLY

I have found that most youth leaders genuinely want to support the vision of their senior pastor. They have great hearts, big dreams and want to make a huge difference for the Kingdom of God. Yet, the reality is that most youth pastors move on after nine to eighteen months.[13] Often they are disillusioned or discouraged.

After more than a decade of speaking to youth leaders, I have been able to compile a list of areas they have identified as their greatest needs.

1. The need for mentoring
2. The need for fathering/mothering
3. The need for finances and resources
4. The need to feel appreciated and valued
5. The need to be included as a part of the church team
6. The need to be stretched and challenged
7. The need to be in a dynamic environment
8. The need for their leadership to keep growing and moving forward
9. The need for accountability
10. The need for their pastor to not be threatened or intimidated by them or their gift

11. The need to be given permission and opportunity to flourish
12. The need to be able to hand on the baton like Elijah and Elisha and an environment that fosters this
13. The need for direction
14. The need for ongoing training and development
15. The need for friends and peers in the ministry

When these needs are being met then you can expect that your youth pastor will be around for the long haul. They need to feel they are supported, and serving in an environment where they can grow and flourish.

When someone does not feel valued, appreciated, or feels stifled and contained, then they will want to find a more nurturing environment to be a part of.

The degree to which we invest in our leaders is the degree to which we will reap the rewards. When the senior pastor has a genuine vision for youth as part of their overall vision for the church, and is committed to seeing it grow, the youth leader will catch this vision and communicate it to the young people of the church.

THE BENEFITS OF A YOUTH MINISTRY

In my experience, most thriving churches have great youth ministries. They have discovered that there are many benefits from investing time, energy and finances into building a great youth ministry and have come to understand the role of the youth ministry in building the church.

Here are some of these benefits:

1. Young people generally have many unsaved friends
2. Young people will bring their friends to church if they love church
3. As a crowd tends to attract a crowd, church becomes the place to be
4. Young people generally have families who can end up coming to church because of the youth program
5. The youth ministry can become the leadership factory of the church. It becomes the training ground for future leaders
6. You build sons and not hirelings when they are raised in the womb of your own youth ministry. They become infused with your churches vision and culture
7. Young people have energy and a zest for life that is contagious
8. Young people have more time and disposable income to put the Kingdom first
9. Young people are generally zealous enough to still believe they can change the world, and the youth ministry begins to foster history makers
10. The availability of the youth ministry stops many young people from going down a path of death and destruction

11. Young people form great friendships
12. Young people are taught powerful life principles
13. Youth ministry provides a great training ground for ministry
14. Young people help keep the church young, relevant, dynamic and vibrant
15. Young people are great servants

However, despite all the obvious benefits, some senior pastors still have objections about youth ministry and its role in the church. I have listed some responses to the most common of these objections.

Objection: We have a young church; we don't need a specific youth ministry.

Response: Your young church will in time become older. Within 10 years, you will miss a generation.

Objection: We had a youth group once but maintaining it was not financially viable

Response: You must take a long-term approach to youth ministry. It will not bring a return immediately, but after years of investing, those same young people will be your best tithers. They will get married and bring their new families to your church.

Objection: Youth just ruin the building and equipment

Response: Be prepared for a degree of wear and tear. A healthy home does not ban the kids from sitting on the couch. However, as we train leaders to take responsibility for things, damage will be kept to a minimum.

Objection: Young people do not tithe so why should we provide a service?

Response: The Gospel is a missionary endeavor, not a money making scheme. The reason God has left us on the planet is to, "Go into the world and make disciples." We need to reach out to the young people in our community not for what they give us but to tell them what Jesus can do for them. (P.S. Teach young people to tithe.)

Objection: The last youth pastor left and took a whole group of young people with them.

Response: We cannot allow the fear of being hurt or used to prevent us from providing a youth ministry. Every endeavor involves some level of risk, but we need to pursue the will of God even if we have been hurt in the past. We must also learn from these mistakes and try to put procedures in place to ensure that, to the best of our abilities, this does not happen again.

Objection: The youth pastors just want to use our church reputation to build their own ministry.

Response: Address this issue with the youth pastor. Ensure that if they are on your team, they are committed to building your church. I encourage you to set reasonable boundaries on how much they are released to pursue outside ministry opportunities.

Objection: The youth church just has its own vision and seems to be working against us.

Response: I believe that if you set appropriate boundaries and address issues as they arise then this kind of scenario does not need to happen. If you have a strong vision that is clearly articulated and agreed upon, you can ensure that you do not have a 'church within a church' culture to develop.

Objection: There always seem to be problems between the parents and the youth ministry.
Response: Ensure that there are strong communication lines between your youth leaders and parents. Also, I encourage you to support your youth leader in front of the parents and your church. With the right training, your youth leaders will learn the importance of fostering strong parent/youth relationships.

Objection: The youth meetings/activities always finish late and take away from the main church programs
Response: Make it clear to your youth leaders that there are time constraints and remind them that everything they are doing should be building the overall vision of the church and not taking anything away from it.

I believe the benefits of investing into the lives of youth leaders and young people far outweigh the objections. As senior pastors, the most important thing to remember is to have a long-term view of youth ministry. It is not about numbers, events, charismatic personality types or overnight success. Building lives takes years of effort, sacrifice and finance. If we commit to building our leaders, they will in turn build our young people. If we treat the youth ministry as a vital part of the church, they will be a vital part of the church.

I encourage you to commit to the generations by investing into the lives of young people. This will ensure the future of the church of Jesus Christ on planet earth.

Epilogue
A Senior Pastor's Perspective

I can clearly remember the Sydney Entertainment Centre filled with thousands of teenagers at the final Youth Alive event for 2001. Hundreds made their way forward to give their lives to Jesus. It was Christine's last public function in her role of Director of Youth Alive New South Wales, and what a fitting finale for someone who is totally dedicated to seeing young people come to Christ.

Events like that one, and leaders such as Christine, are not only impacting the younger generation - they are changing the future. **This is a powerful reason why youth ministry should be a significant part of the vision of every local church. It is all about impacting the generations and changing the future.**

The Word continually speaks of God's eternal plans which span from one generation to another generation.

Psalm 145:4 says, *"One generation shall praise your works to another and declare your mighty acts."*

There is a powerful spiritual link between generations. What we are doing today is building a legacy for those who will come after us.

The older one gets, the harder it seems to understand the next generation. Sadly, some churches have allowed the 'generation gap' to prevail. I have heard some senior pastors say about their youth, "It wasn't like this in our day!"

Yes, young people in the 21st century may appear to be more experimental, eccentric or exteme than any other generation. They like pushing the boundaries, but these are not necessarily bad qualities. If we channel this energy to Kingdom purposes, we will see a radical generation raised up, passionate about serving God.

People presume that the generations are getting worse, but I believe, with the right input, they are getting stronger. I look at young people today and it is obvious they are confident in areas I was not when I was 18. As we commit to building young people, we are building the future.

The older I get the more I recognize the need to trust younger people in positions of leadership. If I was threatened by the popularity of our youth leaders, I would most likely suppress them and try to contain their zeal.

As a senior pastor, I have discovered the value in releasing young people in ministry within the life of our church. Not only do I love seeing them flourish and increase; their enthusiasm inspires me. Young people are an essential part of a healthy, functioning church because they help keep it fresh and relevant.

Christine has given a range of vital keys for becoming an exceptional youth leader and for building a great youth ministry. Yet the central focus should always be the big picture - building the church of Jesus Christ, seeing lives changed, and impacting the generations to come.

There is more opportunity today than ever before for youth ministry to make a significant impact for the Kingdom of God. Big events and youth rallies are instrumental in drawing young people to Jesus, but it is the effective youth ministries of local churches that are building lives. Senior pastors who do not recognize the potential of youth ministry are limiting themselves. Young people are the future of the church.

In this book, Christine has done a brilliant job of putting youth ministry in perspective and describing the DNA of an awesome 21st century youth leader. Any senior pastor would be blessed to have leaders of this calibre.

This book is not only an excellent resource for youth leaders - it is of exceptional value to any senior pastor who is committed to impacting not one generation, but the generations! In my view, this is essential reading for pastors and leaders.

Brian Houston
Senior Pastor - Hillsong Church, Australia

"Youth is not a period of time. It is a state of mind, a result of the will, a quality of the imagination, a victory of courage over timidity, of the taste for adventure over the love of comfort. A man doesn't grow old because he has lived a certain number of years. A man grows old when he deserts his ideal. The years may wrinkle his skin, but deserting his ideal wrinkles his soul."

Anonymous

Thank you to:

Nick - The love of my life, you are the most amazing person I know. Thank you for loving, releasing and supporting me, and always keeping us focused and grounded on the King and His kingdom.

Catherine Bobbie - Your arrival has unlocked a 'love bomb' that was hidden in my heart. I am already insanely in love with you!

Maria Ieroianni- God truly smiled on Nick and me when He sent you to work alongside us. You make our lives possible. Words cannot express my gratitude for the countless hours of editing, writing and layout you have invested into this book. It could not have happened without you. You are a genius!

Pastors Brian & Bobbie Houston - For being the most amazing pastors, and daring to release the generations. I would not be here if it was not for you.

Joyce Meyer - Your incredibly generous support and partnership over the past years has enabled me to share the Gospel with multiplied tens of thousands of young people around the world. Thank you for believing in young people.

Special thanks also to:

Brian Houston; Jeanne Mayo; Mike Hardie; Russell Stefans; Russell Hampson; Rebekah Woodward; Geoff Woodward; Ruth Yallop; Kate Vickers; Daryl-Anne LeRoux, Rexopoulous, Mal Fletcher; Russell Evans; Benny Perez; Reverend Spike; John Morgan; Monica Prescott; Odd Arve Roed; Andreas Nielsen; Aaron Jayne; Jurgen Matthesius; Sam Monk; Dan Meyer, Nancy Alcorn, Wendy Kelly and Flavius Cornelius III.

christine caine

Footnotes

[1] W.A Pratney Communication Foundation

[2] National Church Life Survey

[3] Barna Research Group, 1994

[4] Australian Census, ABS 1996

[5] U.S. Census Bureau

[6] U.S. Census Bureau

[7] 'Before Our Very Eyes: What TV Sex & Violence Are Doing to Us, Ronald Reno, 1995

[8] "Sex on the Web," CNET.com, 1999

[9] W.A. Pratney Communication Foundation, 1999

[10] 2001© Kate Spence/Shout! Publishing

[11] Official Tiger Woods Homepage

[12] "The Tasks of the Youth Leagues", Lenin, 1920

[13] Barna Research Institute

References

- Barna, George, *Baby Busters- The Disillusioned Generation*: Moody Press, 1994
- Coupland, Douglas, *Girlfriend In a Coma*, Harper Collins, 1998
- Hybels, Bill, *Fit to Be Tired:* Zondervan Publishing House, *1991*
- Jones, Tony, *Postmodern Youth Ministry*: Youth Specialities, 2001
- Lenin, V.I, *The Tasks of the Youth Leagues*:1920
- Maxwell, John C., *Developing the Leaders Around You*: Thomas Nelson Publishers, 1995
- Maxwell, John C., 17 *Indisputable Laws of Teamwork*: Thomas Nelson Publishers, 2001
- Maxwell, John C., *The Success Journey*: Thomas Nelson Publishers, 1997
- Watkins, William D., *The New Absolutes*: Bethany House Publishers, 1996
- Zschech, Darlene, *Extravagant Worship*: Check Music Ministries, 2001
- Microsoft Encarta Encyclopedia, 2000
- Sweet, Leonard, *SoulTsunami*: Zondervan Publishing House, 1999

Recommended Reading

- "A Leader's Guide To Youth Ministry", Julia A'Bell, Empower Team, 2002
- "Developing The Leaders Around You", John C. Maxwell, Thomas Nelson Inc, 1995
- "Developing The Leader Within You", John C. Maxwell, Thomas Nelson Inc, 1993
- "Extravagant Worship", Darlene Zschech, Check Music Ministries, 2001
- "For this Cause", Brian Houston, Maximised Leadership Inc 2001
- "Fruit that will Last", Tim Hawkins, 1999
- "Girlfriend in a Coma", Douglas Coupland, Harper Collins 1998
- "Heaven is in this House", Bobbie Houston, Maximised Leadership Inc, 2001
- "Jesus for a New Generation", Kevin Graham Ford, InterVarsity Press, 1995
- "Making God Famous", Mal Fletcher, Next Wave International, 2001
- "Purpose Driven Youth Ministry", Doug Fields: Zondervan Publishing House, 1997
- "Saving the Millennial Generation", Dawson McAllister, Thomas Nelson Inc 1999

- "Student Ministry for the 21st Century", Bo Boshers, Zondervan Publishing, 1997
- "The Pioneer Spirit", Mal Fletcher, Next Wave International, 2002
- "The Power of Story", Leighton Ford, NavPress 1994
- "The 17 Indisputable Laws of Teamwork", John C. Maxwell, Thomas Nelson Inc, 2001
- "Youth Leaders Guide To Sanity", Russell Evans, Planet Shakers Ministry International, 2000
- "Youth Ministry Nuts & Bolts", Duffy Robbins, Zondervan Publishing House, 1990
- "Youth: The Endangered Species" Mal Fletcher, Triune Pub., Word, Australia, 1991
- "Understanding Today's Youth Culture", Walt Mueller, Tyndale House Publishers, 1994

About the Author

Christine Caine is a dynamic and passionate visionary whose poweful testimony of restoration impacts thousands of lives around the world each year. She lives in Sydney, Australia with her husband Nick and daughter Catherine. They are based at Hillsong Church.

As one of Australia's leading communicators and the Director of Equip & Empower Ministries, Christine's inspiring message goes beyond reaching youth. It is also impacting the lives of leaders, women, the wider church and the unchurched across the world

Her vision is to help people overcome the obstacles, hurdles and challenges of life and maximise their God given potential and purpose.

She is a pastor at Hillsong Church, the Coordinator of the Hillsong Network and the Principal of the Hillsong International Leadership College's Evening Program.

She was formerly the Director of Youth Alive NSW and the Director of Hills District Youth Services.

To contact Chris:

email: chriscaine@chriscaine.com
or via mail
PO Box 1252
Castle Hill, NSW 1765, Australia

christine caine

Resources

FURTHER RESOURCES BY CHRISTINE CAINE:

BOOKS

I Am Not Who I Thought I Was

TESTIMONY VIDEO

I Am Not Who I Thought I Was

TAPE SERIES

- You Can Succeed - *Success principles for life*
- Winning Keys - *Keys to winning in life*
- Dare to Win - *Overcoming your limitations*
- Dare to Live - *Living the abundant life*
- Dare to Soar - *Living above your circumstances*
- Relationships - *An issue of the heart*
- Possess the Promise - *Going in to possess your destiny*
- Live to Give - *Giving: the key to living*
- Absolutely Absolute - *Jesus' absolutes*
- Equal But Different - *Men and women, one race; two sexes*
- Chick Speak - *For women aspiring to leadership*
- Youth Ministry - Reality Bites
- Youth Leaders Only
- 21st Century Generation Changers
- Paranormal - *Living beyond the natural*
- The Truth Is In Here - *The Gospel*

For more details about these resources go to:
www.chriscaine.com
or write to:
PO Box 1252
Castle Hill, NSW 1765, Australia